THE
DEADLY
CAMERA

Gordon Snell

POOLBEG

Published 2005
by Poolbeg Press Ltd
123 Grange Hill, Baldoyle
Dublin 13, Ireland
E-mail: poolbeg@poolbeg.com

© Gordon Snell 2005

Typesetting, layout, design © Poolbeg Press Ltd.

1 3 5 7 9 10 8 6 4 2

A catalogue record for this book is available from the British Library.

ISBN 1-84223-241-X

Typeset by Type Design in Optima 10.5/15
Cover design by Steven Hope
Printed by
Cox & Wyman, Reading, Berkshire

www.poolbeg.com

THE
DEADLY
CAMERA

penutse

Also by

About the Author

Gordon Snell is a well-known scriptwriter and author of books for children and adults. Other books in the 'Ballygandon gang' mystery series include *Dangerous Treasure, The Mystery of Monk Island, The Phantom Horseman, The Case of the Mystery Graves, The Secret of the Circus, The Library Ghost* and *Fear at the Festival.* He is also author of *The Tex and Sheelagh Omnibus.* He lives in Dalkey, Co. Dublin, and is married to the writer Maeve Binchy.

For dearest Maeve, with all my love

1

Down to the Harbour

"Get your ugly face out of the way, Dessy, I'm trying to take a picture!" said Brendan, pointing his camera out of the train window. He and his friend Dessy and their cousin Molly were on the DART train in Dublin, going south beside the sea.

Molly's black sheepdog Tina was trying to jump up on to the seat. "Down, Tina, down!" said Molly. "She wants to be in the picture too. Now, Tina, sit!" Reluctantly the dog sat down on the floor and Molly held on to her collar.

They were all on their way to a special ceremony on a new boat in the harbour at Dun Laoghaire.

Brendan's father was a journalist writing about it for his newspaper, and he had got invitations for Brendan and

Molly to go on board with him to look around. They hoped they could get Dessy on board too.

Dessy himself seemed to have no doubts. "I hope this posh boat we're going to see can go faster than those yachts out there," he said. "They're so slow it would take you forever to get anywhere."

"I think they're beautiful," said Molly. "That's the only thing you lot in Dublin have that we don't have in the country – a view of the sea.."

"What do you mean, the only thing?" Brendan always stood up for his city. "We've got movies and bowling alleys and football matches – "

"And crime and traffic jams!" said Molly.

The three of them always enjoyed this running argument about the town and the country. Molly and her family lived in the small town of Ballygandon where her parents ran a grocery shop. Just now she and her mother were staying with Brendan's family in Dublin. She knew that really Brendan and Dessy loved coming to stay with her in the holidays. They called themselves the Ballygandon Gang, and saw themselves as Private Eyes, detecting shady goings-on and protecting the town's landmark, the haunted castle on the hill.

"Do you want to see the picture?" asked Brendan, holding up his camera proudly.

"Sure, when you print it out," said Dessy.

"I don't need to. It's in the camera."

"Of course it's in the camera – do you think I'm an idiot? A hi-tech wizard, that's me. You take a picture with a camera, and the picture is *in* the camera. Hey presto!"

"Shut up, Dessy, you're about as hi-tech as a horse and cart. This is a digital camera, and you can see the picture you've taken by just looking in the viewing screen. See?" Brendan moved beside Dessy and held the camera in front of their faces. Dessy peered at it.

"Wow!" he cried. "It's like a little telly screen. And there I am, Dessy the Handsome Hunk, with the sailing boats in the background."

"And the great thing is," said Brendan, "by zooming in on the yachts and the sea, I can leave you out of the picture altogether!"

"*Very* clever!" said Dessy, losing interest at once. "But tell me this, Mister Whizz-Kid, what happened when the photographer met the crocodile?"

"Tell us, Dessy. We know you're going to anyway," Molly smiled.

"They both took a *snap*, but only the crocodile got any dinner!"

Brendan and Molly groaned. Dessy's fund of bad jokes seemed to be endless. They just hoped he wouldn't try to tell any of them at the ceremony today. The Government Minister who was speaking might not find them funny.

* * *

At Dun Laoghaire station, they got off and joined the crowds going up the stairs to the exit. Outside, they looked towards the harbour and the quays where the ferries docked, and the masts of yachts pointing upwards like tall needles.

"There's Dad!" said Brendan. He pointed towards a big

metal sculpture designed to look like two sails. A tall man in a raincoat, carrying a briefcase, was standing beside it, gazing around him. He spotted them, and waved.

They went across and greeted him. "Hello there," said Brendan's father. He paused, then said without enthusiasm, "And hello to you too, Dessy."

"I knew you wouldn't mind me coming along, Mr O'Hara," Dessy grinned. "The more the merrier, like."

"Usually, yes," said Brendan's father, "but the room on the boat is limited. I had a bit of a job getting them to allow Brendan and Molly to come, let alone your grandfather, who suddenly rang up to say he'd decided to join us for a bit of fun."

"Oh, Locky's coming, that's great!" Brendan and Molly both loved their grandfather, who was full of energy and wild plans for outings. He lived in a place called Horseshoe House, with some other people of his age. It was halfway between Dublin and Ballygandon, and he often paid them visits in his battered old car. His real name was Loughlin, but he'd been known as Locky ever since Brendan and Molly could remember.

"Don't worry about me, Mr O'Hara," said Dessy breezily. "I'll just hang about on the jetty where the boat is parked."

"They say boats are *moored*, not *parked*, you eejit," said Molly. "Even I know that."

"Whatever," said Dessy, "but I wouldn't like the job of clamping them if they *moor* in the wrong place!"

They walked along the road near the harbour, and saw one of the huge white ferries arriving after making the sea crossing from Wales.

"What a boat!" said Molly. "It's as big as a block of flats."

"And fast, too," said Brendan. "They have to slow it down coming into the bay, in case the waves it makes wash away the people fishing off the rocks."

"I'd rather fish in the river in Ballygandon," said Molly.

Brendan took a picture of the ferry boat and showed it to them in the camera screen.

"It stays in the camera with all the rest of the pictures," he explained. "Then later I can look through them and just wipe out the pictures I don't want, and print the ones I like."

* * *

They walked down the wide stone pier that jutted out like a long rugged arm shielding the boats in the harbour. Halfway along they could see a big crowd of people, jostling and chatting and gazing at the large, handsome boat that was moored there. There were triangular coloured flags all along the rigging lines that sloped down from the masts.

On a small bandstand, a fiddler, a guitarist and a flute player were playing. Molly took out her tin whistle and began to play the tune in time with them. The people around them smiled admiringly, though Brendan thought the musicians didn't look quite so pleased.

"Ahoy there, me hearties!" cried a voice beside them. It was Locky. He was tall, with curly grey hair, and wore a jaunty green hat with a little feather in the hatband. He raised his hat in the air as he greeted them. "Is it all aboard yet?" he asked. "I've brought my compass."

"Not yet, Locky," said Brendan's father. "I guess we have to wait for the Minister to arrive."

"That pompous windbag!" Locky scoffed. "Slick Jim Shanahan, the wheeler-dealer from the west. He knows as much about boats as a camel in the desert."

"Not so loud, Locky," said Brendan's father. "I'm supposed to be reporting this, remember. I don't want to be turned away because of you."

"Why is *he* doing the speechifying anyway? He's not the Minister for Oceans, or even streams, as far as I know."

"No, but he's a friend of Gaby Grantham, who owns the boat."

"Oh, the businessman," said Locky. "That explains it. He's got more money than sense, or he wouldn't have lashed out so much on this fancy freighter. It must have cost a fortune. I suppose that's why he called it *Merry Midas*."

"What's Midas?" asked Dessy.

"A king in the olden times," said Brendan. "Everything he touched turned to gold."

"There's the man himself," said Mr O'Hara, looking towards the boat. Just emerging on to the top deck was a man in a smart blue blazer with a cravat at his collar and a white peaked cap with gold embroidery round the sides and the brim.

People in the crowd were pointing at the man, who looked round and smiled as he saw the crowds below on the quayside.

"He looks very pleased with himself," said Molly.

"Yes," said Locky, "he's giving himself a fair welcome!"

Up on the top deck, Gaby Grantham raised his arms in

the air. A small, burly man in a check suit handed him a megaphone.

"Good evening and welcome!" Gaby's voice boomed out, crackling. "It is a great pleasure to see you all at the first appearance here in Dublin of my brand-new and magnificent craft, the *Merry Midas.*" He pointed to the flag flying at the stern. "And I hope," he went on, "to carry the banner of Ireland with pride over the seas and into the harbours of the world."

There was some scattered applause from the crowd. The fiddler on the bandstand began to play the National Anthem.

"Not yet, not yet!" called Gaby Grantham. The fiddler stopped as people chuckled. "We must wait for the Minister to arrive, to perform the opening ceremony."

Locky muttered: "Of course! Sure, that fella would go to the opening of an envelope, if there was free food and drink to be had!"

"Afterwards," boomed Gaby Grantham, "I shall be happy to welcome some of you as my guests to tour the ship and view its amazing amenities and its state-of-the-art technology. Thank you."

As some people clapped, there was a murmur in the crowd as along the jetty came first a guard on a motorcycle, and then a black limousine, followed by two more motorcycles. They stopped just before the boat, as the people made way for them.

A woman with sleek black hair, wearing a grey suit, stepped forward and opened the door of the limousine. "You are most welcome, Minister," she said.

Out of the car stepped a man in a dark suit with a blue

tie and a rose in his buttonhole. His wispy brown hair was blown by the breeze. He smoothed it down, and shook hands with the woman.

"Good evening, Minister!" Gaby Grantham had come down from the top deck and was now standing on the main deck, level with the quayside, where a short gangplank led on to the boat. The Minister flinched slightly, somewhat startled. Gaby Grantham had forgotten to put down the megaphone, and though he was only a metre away, he was blasting his greeting into the Minister's ears.

"That's a poor start," said Locky. But there were much more curious events to come.

2

The Merry Midas

Gaby Grantham handed the megaphone to the man in the check suit, and walked across the gangplank on to the quay. He shook hands with Jim Shanahan and said: "This is an honour, Minister. You are very welcome to the *Merry Midas*."

"My pleasure, Gaby," said Jim Shanahan. "Well, this is quite a tub you've got yourself, eh?"

Gaby smiled thinly. "You'll always have your little joke, won't you, Jim? Do come aboard. Hold on to the ropes, and watch your step on the gangplank!"

The Minister stepped gingerly on to the creaking wooden boards, clutching the ropes which were strung between poles on each side of the gangplank. He stood on the main deck, swaying slightly. Gaby Grantham followed him. People began to surge forward, to get aboard. Gaby took the megaphone again.

"Only those with special guest passes, and the media, in the first group please! After the Minister's speech, we will give you a tour of the ship, and then other groups can follow later. She may be a large craft, but not quite big enough for all of you at once."

Brendan's father produced a special yellow invitation card marked *Press* in big letters. A few other media people, some with cameras, went across on to the main deck.

Brendan's father said: "Now wait here, all of you, and you'll be in the second group. Have you all got the passes I gave you?" Locky, Brendan and Molly showed theirs. Dessy held his empty palms up and shook his head, making a mournful face.

"Sorry, Dessy, I didn't even know you were coming. You'll have to let the others tell you about it."

"No problem, Mr O'Hara," said Dessy.

"I'll take pictures for you," said Brendan.

"And you can look after Tina too!" said Molly.

"Sure," said Dessy. "I can see Tina isn't a 'Sea Dog' anyway!"

Brendan's father went on board, together with some posh-looking men and women who must have been the Special Guests. The Guests were shown to the fixed benches around the rail of the deck, and a few folding chairs. The media people leaned against the rails. The Minister and Gaby Grantham appeared on the top deck where the control tower was.

"You are all welcome to this opening ceremony to mark the first visit of my brand-new craft, the *Merry Midas*, to Dublin. I can hardly call it a launch of the ship, since as you can see, she is launched already, and floating well!" There was some laughter and clapping from the crowd. Gaby went on: "We are privileged to have with us to perform this ceremony, our much admired Government Minister, Mr Jim Shanahan TD. Over to you, Minister!"

Jim Shanahan took a card from his pocket and glanced at it, clearing his throat.

"Well, at least it looks as if he's not planning to speak for long," said Molly.

"I wouldn't bet on it," said Locky. "He can sometimes get carried away and rabbit on for hours."

"Good evening, my friends," said Jim Shanahan, smiling. "It is with the utmost pleasure that I am here today to help to cheer on its way what I may call a flagship for Ireland's business community – a community of which as you know Gaby Grantham is a leading entrepreneur . . ."

"Leading fixer more like," whispered Locky. "A lot of secret money in bribes has passed to and fro in *his* business career, I'll bet."

The Minister went on with his praises of Gaby Grantham and of this new venture, the *Merry Midas.* The audience on the boat listened politely. Brendan's father was making notes of the speech. Cameras clicked, and a TV cameraman was filming. Brendan produced his own camera and took a photograph. He passed round the camera to the others so they could see into the screen. It was a clear shot of the Minister up on the top deck.

11

Then Brendan held it out and looked into it himself, saying: "I can alter the picture in the camera to be close-up or further away."

"Further away is better in his case," said Dessy. "He's a seedy-looking character."

They listened until finally Jim Shanahan ended his speech: "Congratulations to you, Gaby, and to the *Merry Midas* and all who sail in her!" There was applause from the audience on the deck, and some clapping from the crowd on the quayside too.

They heard Gaby Grantham say to the check-suited man: "Larry – the champagne!"

Larry picked up a bottle of champagne from the floor beside him and handed it to Gaby, who passed it to Jim Shanahan, saying; "Will you do the honours, Minister?"

The Minister took it and looked around, puzzled. "I can hardly smash it on the back of the boat from here, like they usually do at launchings," he said.

"I'd rather you didn't try," said Gaby hastily. "Just open it. That'll be fine."

Jim Shanahan fiddled with the cork, and after some help from Gaby in twisting it loose, the cork exploded from the bottle with a loud *Pop!* and flew up into the air. Jim Shanahan suddenly seemed to get over-excited, and began to shake the bottle up and down like the winning team in a motor race. Then he held the bottle up and waved it around, while the liquid squirted out, splashing over the VIP's and the Press on the deck below.

There was laughter and some shrieking.

They heard a piercing voice say: "My new dress is ruined!"

12

Gaby Grantham took the champagne bottle away and said: "Thank you, Minister, for that *bubbly* speech. And now I shall escort the first tour round the delights of this magnificent vessel."

He went down the stairs to join the crowd on deck, followed by the Minister, who was immediately involved in an argument with the woman in the drenched dress.

"This way please, ladies and gentlemen!" said Gaby loudly, as he firmly pulled the Minister away and led him and the group through a door into the inside rooms and cabins.

"I'm going to go along the pier and take some shots of the other boats," said Brendan.

"Yes, Tina could do with a walk," said Molly.

"I'll wait here for you," said Locky, "and mind you're back in time for the next group tour."

"Don't worry, Locky," said Dessy. "We won't be long. Would you like a jelly-baby to keep you going?" He took a sticky paper bag out of his pocket and held it out.

"Thanks all the same, Dessy," said Locky, "but I'll pass on those."

* * *

There were boats of all sizes moored in a great crowd in the inner part of the harbour. Brendan wondered how the owners got to the far ones. Perhaps they stepped across the other boats, or took a little dinghy out to reach them. A lot of the boats were covered in blue canvas tarpaulins stretched across from side to side. As they reached the edge of the landward end of the quay, they saw a big expanse of tarmac like a car park – except that this was a boat park. The boats had been dragged up on to the land ready to be launched when they were needed.

They were near enough to touch, and Brendan undid a metal clip on one of them and lifted the canvas flap. Inside he could just see a hollow area with built-in seats, and at the rear, the rudder the boat was steered by. He saw a man, who was tinkering with one of the boats nearby, glance across at him with a frown. He quickly pulled the flap back, smiled and moved on.

Brendan took some pictures, while Tina snuffled around happily, wagging her tail.

"She's finding some great smells here," said Molly.

"So am I," said Dessy. "The place stinks."

"Nonsense, that's the sea air," said Molly. "You've got too used to the mucky atmosphere of Dublin."

"Sea air and a few rotting fish as well," Dessy said.

Brendan looked back down the pier and said: "I can see the first crowd coming up on deck and starting to get off. We must get back."

They hurried back along the pier in time to find Locky looking at his watch. "I thought you must have fallen into the harbour," he said. "I was just about to plunge in and rescue you."

Brendan's father stepped off the gangplank and joined them.

"On you go," he said. "It's all very luxurious inside. More like a hotel than a ship. I'll just phone some paragraphs in to the paper, and meet you here later."

He took out his mobile phone. Locky, Brendan and Molly were ready to show their passes as they queued up at the gangplank. Molly handed Tina's lead to Dessy.

"Keep a tight hold on her, Dessy," she said.

"Aye aye, Captain," said Dessy. Tina gave a bark. "She says *Aye aye* too," Dessy grinned.

* * *

Gaby Grantham welcomed them aboard and said that his assistant Lavinia would show them around. The woman they had seen welcoming the Minister earlier stepped forward. "Please follow me and keep together," she said sternly. "This way!"

She led the way along the deck beside the raised structure in the middle of the boat. They had to go in single file here, and Lavinia called back: "Take care, please – and mind you hold on to the rail."

They emerged on to another wider section of deck at the front of the boat, which had winches and pulleys around it. The deck was smart, polished wood, and there were ropes lying neatly coiled on it. Looking up, they saw the flag-studded rigging going up to the tall masts above. A small flight of steps led down to a little triangular deck which was pointed at the bow. A pole carved in the shape of a green mermaid stuck out from the bow itself.

Molly and Brendan went down on to the little deck. They saw the hooks of a rope ladder attached to one of the rails near the quayside. On the upper part of the deck, Lavinia was talking to the group, who were staring upwards as she explained the elaborate radar and satellite receivers way above them.

Then they heard a grunt and a curse and a scuffling sound. The noises came from the side where they had seen the rope ladder. They looked across, and saw to their amazement the face of Dessy peering through the railings. "Come on. Help me up!" he hissed.

They rushed across and each grabbed one of Dessy's hands, as he scrambled up and on to the deck.

"Wow, that was close!" Dessy gasped. "I nearly fell in when I jumped for the bottom of the ladder. Look, my feet are soaking wet."

"Where's Tina?" asked Molly. "What have you done with her?" She rushed to the side as though expecting to see Tina swimming around in the harbour.

"Don't worry. She's fine," said Dessy. "I tied her to a post. Look, she's over there." He pointed to the quayside and they could see the dog lying down with her lead attached to a post.

"I must go to her," said Molly.

"No, you'll give Dessy away," said Brendan. "Then we'll all be thrown off."

"What's going on down there?" They heard the voice of Lavinia.

"Get down, Dessy!" whispered Brendan, and Dessy crouched on the deck while Molly and Brendan stood side by side to shield him from view.

"Nothing, Miss – we're just looking around," said Molly.

"Well, come back and join the group. You shouldn't have been down there in the first place."

She turned back to the group and said: "Now please follow me and we shall see some of the elegant staterooms and cabins which are a luxury feature of the *Merry Midas.* She led the way down some stairs and, as the group began to follow, the Ballygandon Gang trooped up to the deck and followed at the end.

"Stop making that sloshing noise, Dessy," said Brendan.

"I can't help it; my trainers are waterlogged."

"Where did you spring from, Dessy?" asked Locky, coming back from the group to look for them. "Out of the ocean, it looks like. And what have you done with Tina?"

"She's OK. Look," said Brendan.

Locky looked across at the dog and grunted. "Your father isn't going to be happy about this carry-on."

"Oh Locky, he doesn't have to know, does he?" Brendan pleaded.

"Well, I suppose not, if we get away with it," his grandfather smiled.

They followed the tour down to the staterooms.

"Why are they called staterooms?" Brendan wondered.

"Because they're always left in a terrible state, like your bedroom!" said Dessy.

"Well, this one is state-of-the-art luxury, I'd say." Locky looked round admiringly. They were in a very large room like a living-room, with a dining-room opening off it at the far end. There was a fluffy white carpet with a big coloured coat of arms woven into the middle, leather sofas and chairs, a huge plasma-screen television, a leather-topped desk with brass handles, low polished coffee-tables, and a cocktail cabinet stacked with bottles and glasses and an ice-bucket.

There were gold-framed paintings on the wood-panelled walls, showing dramatic ocean sailing scenes.

"I could certainly put up with this pad for a while," said Molly, as Brendan took photographs and the group wandered around ooh-ing and aah-ing at everything.

Locky tried a door at the far end of the dining-room. It was locked.

"That's private cabin accommodation," said Lavinia.

"I'm sure it's just as lavish as this," Locky remarked.

"Absolutely!" She turned to the group and said: "Now that ends the tour, so if you'd like to follow me up the stairs again, we shall move back on to the quayside. Thank you."

Brendan, Molly and Locky brought up the rear, huddling round Dessy in the hope that his scruffy appearance and sloshing shoes wouldn't be noticed.

As they went back along the narrow part of the deck, Brendan noticed a circular skylight let into the roof of the cabins below. He leaned over and peered down through it. What he saw made him gasp with astonishment.

3

A Secret Deal

Brendan could see down in the cabin two beds with purple duvets on them, and a wooden locker at the end of one of them. Gaby Grantham was sitting on the end of one bed, and opposite him in a chair at the other side of the locker was Jim Shanahan. The Minister was watching intently as Gaby Grantham counted out a wad of banknotes.

"Come on, Brendan – everyone's getting off," said Molly. "Locky's gone on ahead."

"Just a second!" Brendan took out his camera and pointed it down through the skylight. He could see the scene below clearly through the viewfinder.

He watched Gaby Grantham finish counting one batch of notes, and slide it across the top of the locker. Just as Jim

Shanahan was taking it, Brendan pressed the button. The camera flashed. The two men looked up, startled. Brendan pressed the button again. He saw the Minister stuffing the money into his pocket. Through the skylight he could hear Gaby shout: "Who the hell's that?"

Then Gaby rushed to the door of the cabin and wrenched it open.

Brendan didn't wait to see any more. "Run for it!" he told Molly and Dessy.

"What's up?" Dessy asked.

"Tell you later," said Brendan, as they hurried towards the gangplank.

Just as they stepped on to the quay where Locky was waiting, they heard a clatter behind them as Gaby Grantham came rushing up the stairs. He looked around wildly. "Where is he? Where is he?" he yelled.

Brendan said softly: "He hasn't seen us yet. Slow down and we'll mingle with the crowds."

"What's going on?" asked Locky.

"Don't ask me! Brendan's going crazy, I reckon. Anyway, I'm going to get Tina." Molly went across to the post and untied the dog, who whimpered and barked and jumped up, licking her face.

Brendan could see Gaby Grantham on the deck, talking angrily to Larry and gesturing towards them. "Locky, Dessy, stand in front of me," said Brendan.

"OK," said Locky, as they turned their backs towards the boat. "But what are you panicking about?"

Whispering urgently, Brendan told him what he'd seen.

"It sounds like some kind of shady deal, all right," said Locky.

20

"And it's all here, in the camera!" said Brendan.

"From the fuss they're making over there on the deck, that fella is dead worried," said Dessy.

Molly came over to them with Tina. The dog saw Brendan and jumped up and down at him, licking him and barking with delight.

"Sssh, Tina – good dog, good dog!" said Brendan, stepping backwards and pushing her gently away.

"That's him!" shouted Gaby from the boat, pointing towards them. Brendan had stepped out from behind Locky and Dessy, as he pushed at Tina. Gaby must have seen his face through the skylight, for he called out: "That kid in the green anorak. Grab him! He's a thief!"

"OK, boss!" said Larry, clattering across the gangplank, which rocked and nearly tipped him into the water below.

Brendan was about to run when Locky said: "Brendan, give me the camera. I'll wander off into the crowd. If you don't catch up with me around here, I'll see you back at your Dad's house. But be careful."

"You too, Locky," said Brendan, passing the camera to him. Locky put it in his coat pocket, and strolled casually away into the crowd.

"Come on, we'll walk away quickly," said Brendan, heading down the pier.

"The quicker the better," said Dessy, as they hurried off, with Tina heading the pack. But it was too late.

"Stop, you!" Larry had grabbed Brendan's arm and was twisting it behind his back.

"Let go of me!" shouted Brendan. Tina barked, and scrabbled at Larry's leg with her paws.

5435605

"Get the dog off, or I'll break your arm!" snarled Larry. He looked as if he meant it. Molly pulled Tina away.

People had gathered around the group. "Leave the kid alone!" said a woman. "What's he done?"

"He's a thief!" said Larry.

"What's he stolen?" the woman asked.

Larry was at a loss. He was just obeying his boss's orders. "He pinched a . . . er . . . something from the boat."

"A camera!" It was the voice of Gaby Grantham, who had come up beside them. He looked menacingly at Brendan. "Give it back, you little toe-rag, and we'll say no more about it."

"I haven't got any camera," said Brendan.

"I saw him take it from a shelf in the stateroom," Gaby explained smoothly to the crowd. "But I'll overlook it if he gives it back at once."

"He's lying!" said Brendan. "I didn't take anything."

"Better to come clean, kid, or you could get hurt," said Larry.

"You're already hurting me, you big eejit," said Brendan. Then he winced as Larry gave another wrench to his arm. .

"Please, no strong-arm tactics." It was Gaby's assistant Lavinia who had come to join the group.

"Let go of his arm, Larry. Now, my young lad, if Mr Grantham says you took the camera, then you took it. He is a man of total integrity, and he is being very generous. So just hand it over, and we'll forget the whole thing." She smiled a sickly smile.

"How can he hand it over if he hasn't got it?" said Dessy.

"You keep out of this, you scruffy urchin!" snapped Lavinia.

Dessy looked as if he was about to retaliate, so Brendan said quickly: "Listen, I took nothing, and I've got no camera on me. You can search me if you like."

Larry looked towards Gaby, who nodded. Larry reached towards Brendan.

"You can keep your hands off," said Brendan. "I'll take off my anorak." He took it off and handed it to Larry.

"I'll do that," said Lavinia, taking it, while Larry scowled at her. Lavinia felt in the pockets and brought out a note-book and a pen. She turned the anorak inside out. Meanwhile Brendan pulled out the pockets of his jeans and showed the contents: some crumpled tissues, a few coins, a key, and a packet of chewing-gum.

"He's clean, see?" said Dessy, trying to talk like a gang-ster movie.

"What about him, then?" Larry said gruffly, pointing at Dessy. "That kid could have passed the camera over to his mate."

"You can search me too," said Dessy, beginning to empty his pockets. Out of them he produced some money, his sticky bag of sweets, a broken pencil and a bright green yo-yo. "Would you like a sweet?" he asked Lavinia, holding out the bag.

She wrinkled her face in disgust, and turned to Molly, flicking her fingers. Molly pulled out her pockets, which contained only a green handkerchief, money, an elastic bracelet and her tin whistle. "See – no camera!" She smiled sweetly.

"They must have it somewhere," said Gaby Grantham. "I saw him take it."

"Perhaps the dog ate it!" said the woman in the crowd, grinning.

"There was an old guy with them earlier, I think," said Larry, "a tall fella in a green hat."

"Well, he's not here now," said Lavinia, looking around.

Just then they heard the roar of a motorcycle. It was a guard, and he was followed by the Minister's limousine.

"Here come the cops," said Dessy in his gangster voice. "Let's get them on the case!"

"Shut up!" said Gaby Grantham sharply. "There's no need to bring the guards into this."

The motorcycle and the limousine stopped beside the crowd. The guard asked them to move aside. The driver got out and spoke into a mobile phone: "We're ready to go, Minister."

They saw Jim Shanahan appear on the deck and walk towards the gangplank. The musicians on the bandstand began to play. Gaby Grantham held out his hand to the Minister as he stepped on to the quay. Jim Shanahan shook his hand, but his face looked grim.

Gaby Grantham looked round at the crowd with a broad smile, and said: "I am sure we would all like to thank the Minister for being with us today on this happy occasion."

He clapped his hands. A few people joined in.

Tight-lipped, Jim Shanahan said; "Thank you, Gaby. And thank you, all." The two of them moved towards the limousine. They were just passing Brendan and the others when they heard Jim Shanahan whisper to Gaby: "Did you get the camera?"

"We're working on it."

"You'd better find it or you'll be in trouble!"

"I won't be the only one!" Then Gaby said loudly: "Thank you again, Minister, and goodbye."

The chauffeur opened the door of the limousine. "Goodbye," said Jim Shanahan curtly, and got into the car. The motorcycles revved up and the limousine moved off down the pier.

"Well, we'll be off then," said Brendan. "Thanks for showing us round the boat."

Gaby looked as if he would like to grab him and throw him in the harbour, but he said nothing.

As the three of them walked away with Tina beside them, they heard Gaby Grantham muttering to Larry and Lavinia.

"I hope your father's got his car waiting for us," said Molly. "The sooner we get away from that lot, the better." She looked round. "Hey, I think they're following us. Keep walking."

Brendan and Dessy glanced back as they moved along. In the distance they could indeed see Larry and Lavinia walking after them, pretending to be casual.

"Speed up!" said Dessy. They walked faster, and looked back to see their pursuers quicken their pace too.

"Let's dash ahead and dodge in there among the crowd of boats on the quayside," said Dessy. They began to run, with Tina leaping along happily. They got into the shelter of the boats that had been dragged up on to the tarmac. They peered out and saw Larry and Lavinia go past, towards the entrance to the pier.

"We'll lie low here till we see my dad there, and go and join him," said Brendan. "Even if they see us, they won't be

25

able to do anything."

"At least Locky has got away with the camera," said Molly.

"Well, hello there, folks!" It was Locky's voice. They looked around them, startled.

Then Brendan saw the boat they had peered into earlier. The flap was lifted, and out from it gazed the smiling face of his grandfather.

"Locky!" the three of them exclaimed at once.

"I thought I'd hide out till you got away, to make sure you were all right."

"But Locky, they're after us now. They're catching up with us!" said Brendan. "You must get out and come with us! We'll all get away in Dad's car."

Then they heard voices nearby. "They must be somewhere around here. I saw them dodge in among the boats." It was Lavinia.

"It's too late," said Locky. "If I come out now they'll see me. You go ahead and find your dad. I'll lie low and come back to your parents' house later."

"But Locky . . ." Molly was worried.

"I'll be OK, don't worry," Locky said, and disappeared into his hiding place, pulling down the canvas flap. He was just in time. They saw the face of Larry come round the front of the boat.

"There they are!" he shouted. He stumbled forward towards them, in the narrow space between the boats.

"Let's go!" said Brendan.

They dodged round the other side of the boat, and then squeezed between it and the boat next to it. They could hear

Larry cursing and stumbling after them.

"Go round and cut them off at the other side!" he called to Lavinia.

"Don't you give *me* orders, you oaf!" she shouted.

They could hear her cursing and crashing about, as they nipped and dodged among the boats. Tina was delighted. She barked excitedly, thinking it was all a new game. Larry and Lavinia couldn't match the speed and nimbleness of the Ballygandon Gang, who were soon a good distance from them. They seemed to have given up the chase, but they could hear the pair of them swearing and arguing with each other.

By now they were at the edge of the boat park, at the road which led along to the entrance to the pier. Brendan saw his father there, looking down the pier, and then glancing at his watch.

"There's Dad!" he said. "We can go home with him, and escape."

"All aboard the getaway car!" said Dessy.

Molly was worried. "What about Locky?"

Brendan thought for a moment. "If we tell Dad about him now, he'll want to go back and get him out of the boat."

"And that would blow his cover," said Dessy. "Locky said he wanted to lie low."

"Yes, we'll tell Dad later," said Brendan.

They went on to the road and hurried to meet Brendan's father. He asked where they'd got to, and wasn't very pleased when they piled into the car and asked him to hurry home.

"We'll explain it all on the way," said Brendan.

"You'd better!" his father said, as they moved off. "And by the way, where's Locky?"

"He went off. He said he'd meet us at home."

"That man is so unreliable, you wouldn't believe it!"

"Oh, he'll be fine," said Brendan. He hoped he was right, as he looked back and saw Larry and Lavinia, still peering around among the boats on the quayside.

4

Car Chase

"Did you send in your story to the paper, Dad?" Brendan was in the front seat next to his father.

"I did, but there's really not much in it. No Front Page headlines in Jim Shanahan's waffling, even if it is on a posh boat."

Brendan thought that once they got the camera and printed out the picture, then it could well become front page news. He decided not to tell his father about the photographs just yet. He was sure Locky would be able to lie low and get away all right. Then when he came home later, they would have the evidence in the camera, and a really big story for Brendan's father to give to the paper.

* * *

Locky was certainly lying low. So low that he had to crouch down in the little space at the back of the boat, with the canvas stretched above his head. It was one of the down sides of being tall, he thought: it was hard to fold yourself up into a small area. His shoulders felt stiff, and he longed to be able to stand up and stretch. Perhaps this pair from the boat would get fed up looking for him, and he could sneak away.

He could still hear them moving around among the boats. They must want that camera of Brendan's very badly. Locky put his hand in his pocket just to make sure the camera was still there. He didn't like to start messing around with it to try and look at the photographs. He didn't understand this digital gadgetry. He preferred the old type where you pressed a button and went *Snap!*

He heard Lavinia say: "We're wasting our time; they must have given us the slip. We'd better go back to the boat."

"Gaby won't be too pleased. He certainly wanted that camera. What picture could the kid have taken, to make Gaby want it so bad?"

"Nothing you need to know about, Larry."

"Don't get all snooty with me, missus. I'm Gaby's right-hand man."

"Right-hand *fist* maybe, but not much in the brains department."

"Well, I wouldn't like to say what department *you* take care of!"

"Get lost, you thickhead!"

Locky hoped they wouldn't go on too long with the argument. At this rate he'd never be able to get away. Then he heard something that made him go chill.

"What's this on the pathway here?" said Larry. "Maybe one of them dropped it."

"A key with a piece of leather attached to it," said Lavinia.

Locky felt in his trouser pocket. He pulled out some coins and a car key. He felt in the pocket again. His key to the place where he lived, Horseshoe House, was gone! He must have dropped it, scrambling about among the boats.

He heard Lavinia say: "The leather's got something stamped on it. *Horseshoe House.*"

"Sounds like some kind of a stable," said Larry.

"Whatever it is, it could lead us to those kids and that tall guy – and to the camera! Come on, let's get back to the boat. At least we've got something to show Gaby we're on the trail."

Locky cursed himself. How could he be so careless? He tried to cheer himself up by thinking they wouldn't know where Horseshoe House was. But to be on the safe side, he'd better not go back there just yet. In any case, he had planned to go back to Brendan's family tonight. Once there, he could hand the camera over, and even if Larry and Lavinia found Horseshoe House and went there, it would be nothing but a wild-goose chase.

Locky waited for twenty minutes, then lifted the canvas flap and climbed out of the boat. Oh, it was good to stand up straight again! He stretched his arms upwards and waved them around. Then he moved cautiously to the edge of the

31

boat park and looked up the pier towards where the *Merry Midas* was moored. There were still quite a few people about, but he couldn't see Lavinia or Larry. He took the car key out of his pocket, and made his way towards the pier entrance. His car was parked along the road.

Just as he turned to go towards it, he looked back up the pier again. On the deck of the boat he could just see Lavinia, with a pair of binoculars pointed at the pier entrance. He ducked round the corner, but not before he saw Lavinia turn to someone beside her, and point in his direction. He hurried away.

* * *

Locky was out of breath by the time he reached his battered old car. He went round to the driver's door and opened it. Then looking back up the road, he saw Lavinia and Larry run out of the entrance to the pier and stare up and down the road. Lavinia pointed again. They'd spotted him. He saw them hurrying along the pavement in his direction. If he drove off quickly, he could get away before they found their own car and followed. But it was too late. They were getting into a silver-coloured car parked just near the pier entrance.

Locky shoved the key into the lock and turned it. "Oh, please start, you old jalopy! Good car, good car!" he pleaded, knowing how temperamental it could be. He was in luck. The engine came to life, and he crunched the car into gear, and turned the wheel. He edged out into the road. He drove as fast as he could, which wasn't very fast in the traffic on the coast road.

He turned right to go up towards the main road. At the first crossroads, the lights were red. As Locky waited, he looked in his rear-view mirror. A few cars behind him in the queue at the lights, he could just see a silver car. Perhaps it was some other car, not the one Lavinia and Larry had got into. But he scowled grimly when he saw Larry's head craning out of the silver car's window, and looking down the line of traffic.

The lights changed. The chase was on!

*   *   *

"You're all very quiet," said Brendan's father as they drove towards home.

"I was just . . . thinking about the boat," said Brendan.

"Yes, quite a vessel, wasn't it? The kind of showy ship you'd expect Gaby Grantham to build for himself. Did you enjoy the tour?"

"Yes, it was good," said Brendan.

"We saw all the gear and everything," Molly said, "GPS and all that."

"I bet you don't know what GPS stands for," said Dessy.

"Geographical something," said Molly. "Positioning, I think."

"No, it stands for *Gang Plank Staggers!*"

"You're an eejit, Dessy," said Brendan.

"Stop bickering, you lot," said his father. "Did you get some good pictures with your digital camera?"

"Oh boy, did we get good pictures!" cried Dessy. "Captain Gaby will jump overboard with joy!"

"And that Minister fella will walk the plank!" said Molly.

"What are you talking about?" asked Brendan's father.

"It's a secret," said Brendan. "I was going to tell you when we got home, but since these two blabbermouths have let it out . . ."

He told his father what he'd seen through the skylight, and how he had taken the photographs.

"Are you quite sure that's what you saw? You're not making it all up?"

"Oh, I saw it all right, and their faces too when they looked up. They looked really surprised."

"I'm sure they did." Brendan's father was excited. "Well, as soon as we get home, we'll put the pictures on to the computer screen and print them out. This could be quite a scoop."

"Well, that's the problem, Dad . . . " said Brendan. "We haven't actually got the camera with us at the moment."

"Then where is it?"

"Locky's got it."

"Locky! What did you give it to *him* for?"

Brendan and the others told him all about Gaby sending Larry and Lavinia after them, and how Locky had taken the camera away so that it wasn't found when they were searched.

"That Grantham guy has got a nerve, asking you to turn out your pockets and searching you. I won't let him get away with that!"

"We went along with it so that Locky could get away with the camera," said Brendan. "They were going crazy trying to find it."

"Things could have got real ugly, Mr O'Hara," said Dessy. "Those dudes were mean hoodlums, I'm telling ya!"

"We'll get the camera when Locky comes back home later on," said Brendan.

"Unless they find him first," said Dessy gloomily. "Then he could be in deep trouble."

They wondered where Locky was now.

* * *

As he sat in his car, Locky kept looking into his rear-view mirror. He could still see the silver car in the line, several cars back. The traffic was moving very slowly as they approached the main road. There was no way they could overtake and catch up with him – not yet. But on the main road into the city, it might be a different matter. Locky made a decision.

At the main road traffic lights, instead of turning right towards the city, he turned left to head into the country where there would be more chance of putting on some speed, and then perhaps slipping off down a sideroad and losing them that way.

Looking back, he could see that the silver car had turned left at the lights to follow him. There were still two or three cars between them. Locky wondered when they would put on a spurt to catch up with him. The silver car must be able to go a lot faster than he ever could.

After they had gone nearly ten kilometres, the silver car was still the same distance behind. Locky realised they must be deliberately holding back, perhaps till they reached a

35

more isolated stretch of road. He wondered what they planned to do. Maybe they would move across and make him edge into the side of the road. It was time to act.

When he rounded a sharp bend in the road, where he was briefly out of sight of his pursuers, Locky saw a narrow side-road leading off to the left. He swung the wheel and turned into it, stopping a short way along, beside a hedge. He turned in his seat to look back through the rear window. To his relief, he saw the silver car speed by. He jumped out and went to the entrance to the sideroad. Looking warily round the hedge, he saw the silver car heading away into the distance.

It wouldn't be long before they realised he was no longer ahead of them. Perhaps they might turn back or think he was heading for Horseshoe House, and make their way there. That meant he couldn't go back there. And they would know Brendan's father's address, from the guest lists at the press reception on the boat. It would be too risky to go back towards the city in case they'd have someone waiting near-by to waylay him. Locky wondered where to go. He decided that for the moment the main thing was to keep driving into the countryside, to put as much distance between him and his pursuers as possible.

* * *

"Surely Locky should have been back by now?" said Brendan's mother as they were finishing their supper. I've kept his meal warm for him, anyway."

"Perhaps his car broke down," said Brendan. "It's pretty unreliable."

"Just like its owner," Brendan's mother smiled.

"As he's here, I was hoping he might drive us all back to Ballygandon tomorrow," said Molly's mother. She had invited Brendan and Dessy to come and stay for a holiday with them. They would all be able to go to the big regatta and festival being held soon on Lough Gandon, the lake not far from Ballygandon.

"Can't we wait and see what happens about the pictures?" asked Brendan.

"We'll have to see what they're like," said his father. "If they're as revealing as you say, I'll get them in to the editor at once. We can take it from there. Meanwhile, all we can do is wait for Locky to turn up."

*   *   *

Two hours later, there was still no sign of him.

"At least he could have phoned," said Molly's mother.

"He hasn't got a mobile," said Molly.

"There are still such things as public telephones, you know."

"Well, I'm going to ring Horseshoe House," said Brendan's mother. "He might have rung there."

She came back a couple of minutes later, frowning. "I don't know what's going on. They said they hadn't heard from Locky, but that someone had rung up saying they had found a key belonging to the house. The people at Horseshoe House told them Locky's name and said he was the only resident who was out at the moment. It was strange, but the woman phoning asked them to describe him. Then

37

she said they thought they might have seen him, and if they saw him again they would give him the key. Otherwise they'd post it back."

"Locky must have dropped the key when he climbed into the boat to hide," said Brendan. "Then Larry and Lavinia found it after we'd got away."

"Let's hope they didn't find Locky too," said Molly.

"I'm worried," said Brendan's mother. "He knows we're expecting him home. Surely he'd let us know if he's held up."

Just then the telephone rang.

5

The Hideout

Brendan's father went to answer it. They heard him say: "Locky, it's you! Where are you?" During the conversation, Brendan's father looked very concerned. He snapped questions at Locky: "What did you do? What happened then? How did you give them the slip?"

He told Locky that someone had phoned Horseshoe House and said they had found a key. Then he said: "What do you mean, you're going into hiding?"

Brendan's father listened some more, and said sharply: "Locky, stay on the line. Locky! Wait!"

He held on to the phone for a while, listening. Then he clicked the receiver up and down. Finally he turned to them and said: "It's no good. He's gone. He didn't even say where

39

he was phoning from. Just that they followed him and he'd got away, and now he's going into hiding. He said he would be staying with a friend in the country."

"What friend?" asked Brendan's mother.

"A friend called Ethna, not far from Ballygandon."

"I've never heard of anyone called Ethna."

"Nor have I. But he said he hoped to see you kids in Ballygandon tomorrow."

Brendan, Molly and Dessy looked at one another. They had a good idea what Locky must have meant. It was a coded message specially for the Ballygandon Gang.

"Is he all right?" asked Brendan's mother.

"He said he was, and that he still had the camera safe and sound."

"If he's in Ballygandon, why didn't he go to Molly's house?" she asked.

"I've no idea. That father of yours is a mystery to me sometimes."

"Not just to you, believe me!"

* * *

"As soon as we get there, we'll go straight to the castle. That's where he must be hiding," said Brendan. The three of them were on the train next morning, on the way to Ballygandon.

"Yes, he must have meant the castle the ghost of Princess Ethna haunts," said Molly. "He knew we were the only ones who would realise what he was talking about."

"Imagine Locky in a car chase, with that pair after him! I

40

wish we'd been able to hear all about it when he talked to my dad."

"We'll hear all about it from him today," said Molly.

"I wouldn't fancy spending a night in that castle on my own," said Dessy. "Hey, do you know who comes round to collect your tickets on the Ghost Train?"

"No, Dessy – who?"

"The Ticket In-*Spectre!*"

At that moment, Tina gave a bark.

"You see, the dog has a sense of humour, anyway."

"It's no time for joking, Dessy. We've got to make plans."

* * *

When they got to Molly's house, it was a while before they could put their plans into action. Molly's mother gave them a great welcome, and had a meal ready for them. They said they wanted to go and meet Locky, but Mrs Donovan said if he said he'd meet them in Ballygandon, he must be coming here.

Brendan rang home, but there had been no more word from Locky.

When the meal was over they said they were going out to look around.

"Well, don't be too long," said Molly's mother. "You never know when Locky might turn up."

She went through the door to the shop to help Molly's father. Quickly, Molly got a bag and shoved a couple of the leftover sandwiches into it, with an apple and a can of lemonade. "If Locky's up there in the castle, he's probably starving," she whispered.

* * *

They went down the winding road that led to the hill and the castle. They saw Locky's car parked just off the road in a gateway to a field.

"Locky's getaway car!" said Dessy. "He was great to be able to dodge those villains in that old heap."

"Let's hope he *has* dodged them," said Brendan.

They climbed the steep rocky path up to the ruined castle, with Tina bounding ahead. Climbing through a gap in the broken-down stone wall, they picked their way over the rough ground and through a gap into a large roofless room with a big arched window at one end. At the other end there was a huge stone fireplace in the wall, big enough to stand up in.

"Maybe Locky's sheltering there," said Molly. They went across to it, but the fireplace was empty. Looking up, they could see up the ruined chimney to the sky above.

"Locky!" Brendan called. "Locky, where are you?" His voice echoed back from the ancient walls. There was no answering cry – the only sound was the sighing of the wind blowing through the gaps in the stones.

They went on calling Locky's name, as they wandered among the tumbledown walls and passageways. They came to a courtyard, with a big round tower at one end. There was an entrance to it, and stone stairs leading up into the tower.

"Perhaps he's hiding up there," said Molly. "Let's go up

42

and look." They went to the bottom of the stairs.

"Ladies first," said Dessy.

"Not scared are you, Dessy?" Molly smiled.

"No way." But he didn't sound very sure of himself.

They all remembered that this was Princess Ethna's Tower, the place where she had been found murdered all those centuries ago. The legend said that she had been stabbed in this very tower with the long pin of a silver brooch. She was wearing it to a feast, the night before she was due to marry Fergal, the son of the O'Brien family who lived here. The murder started a feud between the O'Briens and the clan of Princess Ethna's father, which lasted for many years.

Her ghost was said to haunt the castle, and especially this tower where she had died.

Indeed, Ethna's spirit had seemed to be an influence and a help to the Ballygandon Gang in many of their adventures.

"I'll go," said Molly. She started up the winding stairs, which were slippy with damp and moss. The walls were clammy as she put out her hand to steady herself. She knew that near the top the stairs had collapsed, so that they ended in empty air, and anyone going on further would plunge down on to the flagstones far below.

As she came towards the final stair Molly felt dizzy. She put her back against the curved wall, her hands splayed out beside her. She felt a strange chill in the air around her.

"Molly, are you OK?" Brendan's voice called from below.

"Fine," Molly called back, steadying herself against the wall. "Locky's not up here. I'm coming down."

"Good searching, Molly," said Dessy.

"But no result," she replied. "Where can Locky have got to?"

"You don't suppose he's starved to death or anything?" Dessy wondered.

"That's right, Dessy," said Brendan. "Cheer us all up."

They went on rambling through the castle, calling Locky's name. After a while they had gone right through the place, and were outside the main walls. Beyond them was what was left of the outer wall, running round the top of the hill.

"What was that?" said Brendan suddenly. "I thought I heard a voice, over there towards the wall. A kind of a whimper, like someone saying: *"Here . . . Here . . ."*

"Yes, I hear it too!" said Molly.

They listened. Now they all heard it, a faint cry that seemed to come from somewhere in the wall itself.

Tina must have heard it too. She gave an excited bark, and ran towards the wall. She began scrabbling in a little hollow under one of the stones. They rushed over to her. They could hear the voice more clearly now: "I'm here . . . I'm here . . . "

"It's Locky!" cried Brendan and Molly together.

"Where are you, Locky?" shouted Brendan.

The voice came back: "In here, in the passage. I'm blocked in."

"Of course!" said Brendan. "I didn't recognise it till now, with all the rocks that have fallen down. This is the entrance to the secret passage, the one that led right through the hillside and came out in the cellar of the library. If we can shift this stone where Tina's digging, we can get inside."

They all began pulling at the stone, and finally eased it

aside to make a gap wide enough to squeeze through.

"We're inside, Locky!" said Molly. "We'll be with you soon."

They crept along the narrow passageway, crouching down so as not to hit their heads on the low roof. They turned a corner and found they were in almost complete darkness now, with just a little daylight filtering in from behind them. They felt their way along the damp sides of the passageway.

"Hello there!" It was Locky's voice just ahead of them, and as he spoke a light suddenly came on. It was a torch beam shining towards them, from behind a large boulder. They could see a figure crouching in the shadows. "Thank God you found me," said Locky. "I thought I was a goner, trapped in here."

Looking over the boulder, they could see Locky. He had a rug wrapped round him, and his hat pulled down to keep his head warm. "Oh boy, am I glad to see you! The Ballygandon Gang to the rescue, eh?"

"We knew you must be here, from your message on the phone," said Molly. "But what happened?"

"I got away from that lot when they followed me in their car, and headed off down the country roads. I decided not to go to your house, Molly, as I was afraid those people might catch up with me. So I decided to hide out here. On my way I rang you from a phone box outside the town. I knew you'd understand the message, and keep it a secret. Then I came up to the castle, and remembered the entrance to the secret passage. I clambered into it, and came this far, bringing the rug and some chocolate I had in the car. I was just settling down for the night when I heard a rumbling sound, and that rock crashed down from the roof, blocking the passage. There was no way I could move it, or get through the gap. I just had to wait and hope."

"I brought you something to eat," said Molly, getting the sandwiches and lemonade from her rucksack and pushing them in through the gap.

"You're a great girl," said Locky, munching hungrily.

"We'll have to try and shift that rock," said Brendan. They all three pulled at it, while Tina barked encouragement. But it wouldn't move.

"We'll have to get a hammer and a metal stake and bash at it, to try and chip away more of an opening," said Molly. "I'll go and find them – I can borrow them from the tool shed behind Morton's Garage."

"Won't Morton be suspicious?" asked Brendan.

"With any luck he won't ever know I've borrowed them," said Molly, moving back down the passageway.

"Well, this is a great picnic," said Locky. "Would any of you like a bit of sandwich?"

"OK, if you're sure you don't want it all . . . " said Dessy, reaching towards the gap.

"Hands off, Dessy, you greedy fool," said Brendan. "Locky needs to build his strength up."

"Sorry," said Dessy. "I'll have one of my sweets. Would you like one, Locky?" He held out the sticky bag from his pocket.

"Er . . . no thanks, Dessy," said Locky.

"You did wonderful work, saving that camera, Grandad," said Brendan. "We'll get a print-out done as soon as we get you out of here. Can I have a look at the camera?"

"Well, that's a bit of a problem," said Locky. "I haven't got it."

They stared at him in shock.

6

The Lost Camera

"You haven't got it?!" Brendan was horrified.

"Well, it's here somewhere but I put it up on a ledge near the entrance to the passageway," said Locky, "so it wouldn't get damaged as I made my way in. Once I was settled I was going to go back and bring it in with me. Then the big rock fell down and I couldn't get back. I hope some bird hasn't flown away with it, or some rat hasn't chewed it – or maybe it's got all damp during the night or –"

"I'm sure it's fine, Locky," said Brendan, though he was far from sure it would be.

"I'm so sorry," said Locky. "I'm an old eejit."

"No, you're not! You couldn't help the rock falling. And you saved the camera. Now all we've got to do is find it."

"It's not on any ledge up there, as far as I can see," said Dessy. "That big boulder must have brought a whole lot of other stones down with it. Look, there's a pile of them at the entrance."

"We'll just have to sift through them," said Brendan. He tried to sound hopeful, but his heart was heavy. Suppose they couldn't find the camera among the rubble – or it had been smashed by the stones? He forced himself to grin. "Come on, Dessy. Don't just stand there. Let's make a start."

They knelt down in front of the pile of stones near the entrance. Dessy began flinging them aside.

"Gently does it," said Brendan. "We don't want to damage the camera."

"It could be banjaxed already."

"That's it, Dessy! Look on the bright side!" But Brendan knew he might be right.

They began painstakingly shifting the tumbled stones aside, while Tina snuffled around, eager to be part of the action. Then suddenly she barked and ran off excitedly. She had spotted Molly, who was just clambering over the wall further along. She was carrying a metal spike and a big hammer. Tina leaped up at her, squealing with pleasure and licking her face. Molly rubbed her head affectionately.

"Hi there!" she called to them. "I've got the gear." She waved the hammer and spike as she walked over. "We'll soon have Locky out of there!"

"Great," said Brendan, "but there's a problem."

He told her about the missing camera.

"We'll do a big search," said Molly, "but first we must free Locky." She went to the boulder and looked through the gap.

49

"Hi, Locky. I've got the hammer and spike. We'll soon have you out of there. Dessy, hold the spike on the rock there, and I'll bash it with the hammer. You'd better keep well clear, Locky. There'll be splinters of rock flying about."

"I'll take a turn with the hammer soon," said Brendan. "Meanwhile, I'll keep searching."

He went back to the pile of stones and went on burrowing. Dessy took a turn with the hammer, then Brendan. Gradually they chipped away at the boulder, and chunks of rock flew off it. The gap widened.

Molly was kneeling at the pile of rocks. She thought it could take hours of rummaging to move them all. And like Brendan, she feared that if they ever did find the camera, it would be damaged and the pictures would be ruined.

Tina beside her was snuffling and panting. Occasionally she would pick up a small stone and run off with it, looking back in the hope that Molly would chase her. When there was no reaction, she came back to the pile of stones. Then she began to bark. She put her nose into a hollow among the stones.

Molly peered at it. Inside, within the higgledy piggledy pile, she could see a glow of light. It had a purplish tinge. As she looked, the light seemed to pulsate, getting brighter and dimmer in a regular rhythm. It was as if someone was signalling.

"Brendan! Dessy! Take a look at this!" They stopped their hammering and came to see.

"There's a light in there. See it?" said Molly.

Brendan knelt down. "You're right. It's inside the pile, among the rocks."

"Perhaps they're on fire," Dessy suggeste

"It doesn't look like flames."

"Then what can it be?" Just then they heard a w.
sound, like the wind screeching through gaps in the ston.
Yet the air was perfectly calm. The sound got louder, and at
the same time the throbbing light in the pile of stones
seemed to get brighter.

"Perhaps it *is* a signal!" whispered Molly.

"Who from?" asked Dessy.

"You know whose place this is . . ."

"Princess Ethna's . . . " Brendan's voice was soft.

"She's helped us before."

"Are you all right out there?" Locky's voice called from
down the passageway.

"Fine!" Molly called. "We'll be with you again soon. We
may have found something."

She reached in among the stones, gingerly taking out a
few, one by one. She could see the glow getting brighter.
Then slowly she extended her arm and felt around inside the
pile with her fingers. Looking in, she could see what the
glowing light was coming from. It was the camera! She
stretched further, and was able to clutch it between her
finger and thumb. Very slowly, so as not to dislodge any
stones, she drew her arm out.

"We've got it!" She held up the camera. As she did so, the
glow faded away, and at the same time the whistling sound
died out.

"Let's have a look at it," said Brendan. He took the camera and turned it around in his hands. "It seems to be OK. A
couple of scratches, that's all." Then he looked into it and

51

clicked the button. "The pictures are all there! We've saved them!"

"With a little help from our friends," said Molly, smiling around at the ruins.

They went to show Locky the camera. "Well, that's a relief!" he said. "I really thought I'd let you down this time."

"You'd never do that, Locky," said Molly. "You're part of the Ballygandon Gang! Now, let's get hammering and let you out of there."

After ten more minutes, they had cut away enough rock to make the gap much wider. Locky was just able to scramble through it. Brendan and Dessy held on to his shoulders as he finally eased his long legs through, and dropped down on to the ground.

"I've had enough of hiding-places!" he exclaimed. "First squashed into that boat, and then walled up in a cave in the rock. Give me the open air, any time!" He stretched his arms and took several deep breaths.

"You're just great, Locky!" said Dessy, giving him a high-five salute.

"You too, Dessy. You know what I missed most, hiding in that cave? Dessy's jokes!"

"A likely tale," said Molly.

But Dessy grinned and said: "Hey, Locky, do you know what they called the crocodile who swallowed a telephone?"

Brendan said sharply: "Dessy, we haven't got time to fool about. We've got to get out of here and print those pictures."

As they began to move away, Locky said: "Dessy, I've got to know the answer."

"A Croco-*Dial!*"

Brendan hissed: "Quiet!"

"Oh come on, it wasn't that bad," said Locky, smiling.

"I mean, stop and stay quiet," said Brendan. "I thought I heard voices."

They listened. They heard someone say: "This is one of the places they often come to, fooling around with their ridiculous games."

They recognised the voice. It was Mrs O'Rourke, the local owner of the holiday caravans based in Ballygandon. She had been involved in various schemes and scams of a very dubious nature, most of which the Ballygandon Gang had been able to help to foil. What was she up to now, they wondered, and who was she with? The best thing was to keep out of her way until they could find out.

"Quick, we'll hide in the entrance to the passageway!" said Molly. She clutched Tina, and they all scurried back into the passageway. They peered out listening. They heard Mrs O'Rourke and another woman talking.

"Well, I hope this isn't a wild-goose chase," said the woman. "I'm not dressed for scrambling about among ruins."

Locky whispered: "I'd recognise that sneery voice anywhere. It's that woman Lavinia, who was trying to hunt me down."

"What can she be doing here with Mrs O'Rourke?" Molly wondered.

"She's up to no good, you can bet on that," said Brendan.

"It's a certainty!" said Locky.

The women's voices were getting nearer.

"OK, we know from that girl's mother in the grocer's that those kids are in town somewhere," said Lavinia, "but no one has seen the old guy."

"He's bound to have come to join up with them," said Mrs O'Rourke. "They go around in a pack. He's like a kid himself."

The Gang looked at Locky, grinning. He gave a great smile, delighted.

"Well, he certainly wasn't at Horseshoe House when we called there," Lavinia said, "and when his friend there said he often went to Ballygandon, I remembered that was where you lived."

"Yes, it's been a long time since that holiday villa scheme of ours was exposed and scuppered."

"Good while it lasted, though."

"Oh yes, and profitable." They both chuckled, and Mrs O'Rourke went on: "And there'll be a profit for me in this too, I assume?"

"Well . . . yes," said Lavinia hesitantly. "I imagine Gaby will see you are taken care of – once we find that camera."

Brendan gripped the camera in his hand. He smiled at the others. Then they heard Lavinia say: "What's that, on the ground there?"

"Where? Oh, this. A bag of sweets. Look!"

"Don't hand it to me. It's all sticky. Ugh!"

"It looks as if those kids have been up here, anyway."

"And scattering stones around, by the look of it. What's this? Some kind of cave?"

The pair were just coming to the entrance.

"It used to lead to a passageway of some kind, I think,"

said Mrs O'Rourke, "but it's all fallen in now."

"Round the corner!" whispered Brendan. They all backed down the passage where it turned the corner sharply. They couldn't be seen if anybody looked in to the cave. Unless they decided to come further in . . .

The Ballygandon Gang held their breath. Then they sighed with relief as they heard Lavinia say: "Well, I'm not going in there. My clothes are dusty enough as it is."

"Well, we know they're around somewhere. You can come and wait at my place if you like."

"I have to get back to Gaby Grantham in Dublin. If you spot the old guy here, try and get the camera from him some-how. But let me know, anyway. We've got to find him. I left Larry watching Horseshoe House in case he shows up there."

"If he's in Ballygandon," said Mrs O'Rourke, "I'll track him down, don't worry! He'll be no match for *me*!"

Locky scowled and shook his fist.

"Well, let's get out of here," said Lavinia.

They heard the voices go off into the distance.

"We'll give them time to go down," said Brendan, "and then we'll take the camera with us to the library. We can print the pictures from their computer."

"But what about Locky?" said Molly. "If Mrs O'Rourke sees him, he could be in trouble."

Picture Problems

Locky smiled and shrugged his shoulders. "Well, it's a sure thing that she won't come up here again looking for me. So why don't I stay?"

"Oh, Grandad, we couldn't ask you to spend another night in that grotty old passageway," said Molly.

"Why not, if it's going to help? It's not exactly a luxury hotel, but it's amazing what you can put up with if you have to."

"Hey!" said Dessy. "Why don't I stay with Locky to keep him company, while you go down and sort out the photographs?"

"Thanks, Dessy," said Locky. "I'd really like that. You and I can have a joke competition."

"And it's *you* Mrs O'Rourke is looking for," said Brendan.

"So it won't matter if she sees us. She knows we are around anyway."

"We'll bring you more rugs and flasks and food and stuff later on," said Molly.

"We could do with a telly as well, eh Locky?" said Dessy.

"Maybe you'd like a snooker table too?" asked Molly.

"Game ball," said Dessy.

* * *

Brendan and Molly made their way down the hill, with Tina running ahead. They walked along the little road leading to the town. Then suddenly Tina went bounding ahead. They saw her snapping and snarling in the gateway to a field. It was where Locky had left his car – and round behind it they could see a figure. It was Mrs O'Rourke, wrenching at the door-handles of the car.

She stopped to shout at Tina: "Get away, you horrible cur! Get away!"

"Tina, come here!" called Molly as they approached. The dog came to her and she snapped its lead on. Still Tina pulled at it, growling at Mrs O'Rourke.

"You should keep that wretched dog under control!"

"She remembers that time you tried to kick her, Mrs O'Rourke," said Molly.

"What were you doing with the car?" Brendan asked.

"Just trying to get into it, to move it out of the way. It's blocking the gate to the field."

"Nobody uses that gate. There's another way in," said Molly.

"Well, it's causing an obstruction. You know whose it is, don't you?"

"No, I've no idea," said Brendan.

"Oh yes, you have!" Mrs O'Rourke glared at them. "It's your grandfather's, isn't it? I've seen him clattering round the town in it, often enough. He's a menace. He should be put off the road. Where is he, anyway?"

"We haven't seen him," said Molly.

"I don't believe you, but when you do see him, tell him I want to meet him, urgently."

"Why?" asked Brendan innocently.

"It's none of your business! Just tell him, will you?"

"Of course," Molly smiled sarcastically, "anything you say, Mrs O'Rourke."

"And keep that horrible dog away from me."

"Yes, Mrs O'Rourke. Come on, Tina."

They walked on up the road towards the town, with Mrs O'Rourke looking after them.

"We've got to get to the library," said Brendan, "otherwise we could have hung around until she left. I hope she won't damage Locky's car."

"It's pretty much of a wreck already," Molly smiled. "In any case, it will distract her from us."

"And she certainly won't find the camera in it!" said Brendan, gripping it in his pocket.

They came to the main road. Molly glanced back and said sharply: "Look out! That dreadful woman is following us."

Indeed, Mrs O'Rourke was coming up the road behind them, moving quickly.

"We'll have to hurry," said Brendan, starting to run.

Molly and Tina followed him. "She doesn't know we've got the camera," said Molly. "She probably thinks we'll lead her to Locky. Let's dodge down some of the sidestreets to get to the library. That way we'll lose her."

* * *

They were out of breath when they reached the library, and rushed in past the librarian, Joan Bright, at the reception desk.

"Hello there!" she said. "*You're* in a hurry!"

"Can we use the computer room, please?" asked Brendan

"Of course," said Joan Bright. "It's open. But what's the rush?"

"We'll explain," said Molly, as they opened the door of the computer room and went in.

Joan Bright followed. "You know dogs aren't strictly allowed in the library, don't you?"

"Sorry, Miss Bright," said Molly, "but it's an emergency. We can't tie her up outside or Mrs O'Rourke would know we're in here."

"Mrs O'Rourke?" Joan Bright was baffled. She decided to give up trying to understand what they were going on about. "All right, you can bring the dog in, just this once. But keep her on the lead."

"We will. We will. Sit, Tina!" Luckily Tina obeyed, as Brendan and Molly sat at the computer.

"Well, I'll leave you to it," said Joan Bright, and went back into the library.

Brendan fiddled with the camera. He produced a square of black plastic and held it up for Molly to see. "There are the pictures," he said, "All in there, safe and sound in this picture-card."

"There's no actual film then?"

"No, all the pictures are digitally recorded in here."

"Amazing."

"That's modern technology!"

"But how do you get the pictures out?"

Brendan rummaged in his hold-all. "I've got the interface link here." He took out a small silver-coloured box. "Now, let's find the cable socket on the computer . . . " He began to look and feel around at the base of the computer and then at the side.

Suddenly Molly whispered: "Brendan – look! On top of the machine."

He looked up. Peering at him, just a few centimetres away, was a pair of yellow eyes. They were set in a black, furry, whiskered face.

"It's Internet, the library cat!" said Molly. "She sleeps in the computer room a lot of the time, don't you, puss?" She stroked Internet's head. Then she took her hand away quickly as the cat bared its teeth and gave a piercing hiss. Its fluffy fur was sticking up in anger. Brendan thought it looked more like a hedgehog than a cat.

"Don't hiss at me, Internet. I'm your friend," said Molly.

"She's not hissing at you," said Brendan. "Look at Tina." On the floor, Tina was staring up at the cat and giving a low growl.

Molly bent down to hold her. "It's all right, Tina. It's only

Internet. She won't hurt you."

Just then the cat leaped from the top of the computer and landed on Tina's back. The dog gave a yelp of pain. Internet jumped off her and began to run round the room. Then she came back and sat down just in front of Tina, pawing towards her menacingly. It was all Molly could do to hold on to Tina's collar, while the dog snarled and yapped.

The door opened. "What's going on?" asked Joan Bright. She took in the scene at once. "Now you see why dogs aren't allowed!" she cried, as she bent down and swooped Internet up into her arms. "There, there, puss-cat, you're safe now. Molly, you'd better get that dog outside right away."

"I'm sorry, Miss Bright," said Molly. "Come on, Tina." She dragged on the dog's lead and brought her out into the hall-way. Tina was turning her head back towards the computer room and barking loudly.

"You'll have to tie her up outside," Joan Bright called. Molly went out and tied Tina's lead on to the railing outside the library.

"Good girl, Tina," she said, giving her a dog biscuit from her pocket. "Wait there. We won't be long."

"Thanks, Molly," said Joan Bright. "By the way, are you getting ready for the festival regatta at Lough Gandon? You'll be in with a good chance in the angling competitions, I'd say. And there's rowing and sailing and all kinds of other events too. We must make sure Ballygandon is well repre-sented."

"Oh we will, Miss Bright!" Molly went back into the computer room.

"There," said Brendan, "I've hooked up the interface and

the camera. Now, here goes!"

On to the computer screen in full colour came a group of pictures. Brendan pointed his finger and then ran it along the first row. There were photographs of Gaby Grantham's boat, inside and out, and of Molly and Dessy and Locky posing on the quayside in front of it.

"Don't we just look as if we owned it?" Molly laughed.

"You do indeed," said Brendan. "Now, there we are! Look there!" He pointed at a picture in the middle of the third row. Molly peered at it. She could clearly see from above the heads of Gaby Grantham and the Minister, Jim Shanahan, crouched over the locker. Gaby Grantham seemed to be counting out notes and passing them across to the Minister.

"You can't see exactly who it is, that's the trouble," said Molly.

"But look at the next one!"

"Oh, wow!" Molly exclaimed. The picture was taken from the same angle, but this time both the men were looking upwards, straight at the camera. They had been startled by the flash when Brendan took the first shot, and looked up to see where it came from. Brendan had clicked the camera again, and there were the faces of the pair of them, clear as could be, and looking very alarmed.

"That will nail them!" said Brendan. "Look, I can enlarge it. There they are in all their glory!"

"A pair of crooks," said Molly. "What do you reckon the money was for?"

"A pay-off, I suppose," said Brendan. "Maybe for Jim Shanahan putting all that government funding into building Gaby's boat."

"You can tell from their expressions it's a secret deal," said Molly. "They both look as guilty as hell."

"Now all we've got to do is to print it out," Brendan said. "Then we'll ring my father and arrange to get it to him. Locky can drive us up to Dublin with it."

He turned on the printer that was linked to the computer, and clicked the *Print* button on the screen. The printer whirred and clonked. Eventually a piece of paper emerged slowly. Brendan picked it up. They looked at it in dismay. The picture was all smudged and blurred.

"That's hopeless," said Brendan. "We'll try again."

But the second picture was just as bad as the first.

"I'll call Miss Bright," said Molly. "Maybe she can fix the printer."

But Joan Bright couldn't help. "I'm afraid that printer has been on the blink for a few days. I've tried changing the cartridge and everything, but it still smudges the paper. Our technical friend, Johnny, is meant to come and sort it out soon."

"Could you ring him, do you think?" asked Brendan. "This is really quite urgent."

"What are you doing exactly?" Joan Bright looked at the enlarged photograph on the screen. "Isn't he that Minister fellow – Shanahan, isn't that the name?"

"It is indeed," said Brendan. He and Molly explained where the picture had been taken, and why they needed to print it out so urgently.

"I'll go and and phone Johnny right away," said Joan Bright.

When she had gone, Molly said: "Maybe we can find

63

some other computer in Ballygandon that we could use."

"Who might have one?"

"Well, my parents haven't, though I've been at them constantly to get one," said Molly. "I suppose Mrs O'Rourke might, but we certainly can't ask *her.*"

Joan Bright put her head round the door. "Johnny's not in at the moment. I've left a message for him."

"Thanks," said Brendan. "We'll just have to keep trying."

"I'm sorry," said Joan Bright. She closed the door and went back into the library.

Brendan began to check the cables between the computer and the printer.

"What's that?" said Molly suddenly. She pointed at the screen. The picture had begun to glow with a purple colour, just like the camera in the pile of stones.

Gradually they saw the single capital letter *E* in white appear on top of the picture, taking up most of the screen. It began to flash on and off. There was a faint sound, too – a long-drawn-out *Eeeeee . . .*like the letter itself.

"What did you do to the computer?" Molly asked.

"I'm not touching it. See?"

They stared at the image on the screen for a while. Still the *E* flashed on and off, and the eerie sound continued. Molly and Brendan looked at one another.

Then Molly said softly: "I think it's a message for us."

"A message?" Brendan's eyes were wide. "You mean, from . . ."

"Yes. From Princess Ethna!"

8

On the Front Page

They both remembered how the spirit of Princess Ethna seemed somehow to have helped them before, with coded messages on the computer screen which had led them in this very library to solve the theft of the Princess's diary. Was it possible that now she was giving them a message about what to do? It might seem unbelievable, but they were convinced that's what was happening.

The *Eeeee* sound was becoming more high-pitched, and the letter was flashing on and off more quickly on the screen, almost as though Ethna was becoming impatient with them.

"But if it *is* a message, what does it mean?" Molly wondered.

"Well, I suppose *E* could stand for *Ethna*," said Brendan. The screen went on flashing. Then they saw something else on the screen. It was a small square, which started from a little box on one side, and then fluttered up and across into a small box at the other side. Another square followed it, then another.

"That's the sign the computer makes when you're sending a file from one place to another," said Brendan. Then he cried: "That's it!"

"What's what?" asked Molly.

"The *E* stands for *E-mail*! The message is telling us to send the picture by E-mail! What a great idea. Why didn't I think of it before? I'll send it to my father that way. I'll go and ring him and then he'll know to wait for it."

He went out into the library to ask if he could use the phone. Molly watched the *E* still flashing on the screen, but the pace seemed to have slowed down again, and the sound got less screechy.

Brendan came back and said his father would be waiting to access the picture on his computer, in the newspaper office. He could print it out there, and if it really was as good as Brendan said, it would be in the paper next day.

Brendan set to work at the keyboard, dialling up his father's E-mail address. The flashing *E* disappeared from the screen, and the sound faded away. Brendan wrote a short note and made the picture into an attachment to the letter. He pressed the *Send* icon, and very soon a message came on to the screen telling him the letter had been sent to his father's address.

"I'll ring and check that he got it," said Brendan, going

out to phone.

Molly looked at the computer screen. She sat down at the keyboard. Just for fun, she typed the words: *Thanks a million, Princess Ethna!* She wondered if the message had somehow whizzed into cyberspace and reached its destination. It didn't seem very likely. But then she saw new words appear on the screen in front of her: *OK. Any time!* Then there was a curious sound from the computer. It seemed strange, but Molly thought it sounded like a chuckle!

Brendan was as startled as Molly when she told him. Then he said: "Well, it worked all right. Dad's got the picture and he says it's terrific. It will be in the paper tomorrow, with a story asking what this payment could be for, and demanding an explanation from the Minister."

"Good work, Brendan. Well done!"

"It wasn't just me. It was all of us. You, and Dessy, and Locky . . . and of course . . ." He glanced at the computer screen and smiled. The screen had gone blank now.

"We can go straight up to the castle," said Molly, "and tell Locky and Dessy the coast is clear. Locky will be glad not to be spending another night up there."

Brendan gathered together his equipment and the camera and put them in his hold-all. Molly began to open the door into the hallway of the library. Then she said: "Wait!"

"What's up?"

Molly whispered: "Mrs O'Rourke is at the reception desk, talking to Joan Bright."

"She must have seen Tina outside."

They saw Joan Bright glance across to the door of the computer room. She saw Molly and gave a quick smile.

67

Then they heard her say: "Yes, that *is* Molly's dog, Tina, so she must be around somewhere. Why don't you have a look in the library? They're probably looking for a book to borrow."

Mrs O'Rourke grunted, then went into the library. Molly and Brendan moved quietly out of the computer room and across the hallway towards the outside door. Molly looked at Miss Bright and gave the thumbs-up sign. The librarian made the same gesture back.

They hurried out of the main door, and Molly untied Tina.

As they walked quickly away down the street, Molly said: "That was close. Thank goodness Joan Bright helped us get away. She realised we didn't want to see Mrs O'Rourke."

"She doesn't get on with her either."

They stopped at Mrs O'Regan's newspaper shop to order six copies of tomorrow's paper.

"What's so special about tomorrow?" Mrs O'Regan asked. "Got your picture in the paper, have you?"

Brendan smiled happily. "It's *my* picture, but it's not a picture of *me*."

"You young people talk in riddles. Anything else?"

"Let's get some doughnuts to celebrate," said Molly. "We can take some to Locky and Dessy too."

* * *

"Food supplies at last!" said Dessy. "I'm starving."

"Thanks a lot," said Locky, munching cheerfully. "It was pretty bleak up here at base camp as we waited to climb to the summit of Everest."

"Locky's been making up his adventures mountain-climbing," said Dessy.

"What do you mean, 'making up'?" said Locky. "Anyway, it was a nice change from your jokes, Dessy."

Molly and Brendan told them how they had got the pictures on to the screen, and sent them by E-mail to Brendan's father in the newspaper office.

"And it was all down to someone who hangs around not too far from here," said Molly, gazing around the ruins.

"Well, I think *I've* hung around here long enough," said Locky. "I could do with a hot bath and a lie-down at your house, Molly."

"No problem. My parents will be delighted to see you."

They clambered over the ruined wall and made their way down the hill. On the road they came to Locky's car parked in the gateway to the field. They told him about the meeting with Mrs O'Rourke.

Locky examined it. "Well, she doesn't seem to have done much damage. A few scratches where she tried to force a window, that's all. She wouldn't have had much joy if she'd tried to steal it. It's hard enough to start, even with the key!" He opened the door and said: "Well, jump in, folks! I can give you a lift."

Locky was right about the car. It hiccupped and gurgled as he turned the key several times.

Finally it started, and they were on their way home.

* * *

Over a meal, they told Molly's parents about sending the

pictures to the newspaper.

"You'd need to be a bit careful, offending people like that," said Molly's father cautiously.

"We will, dad," said Molly. If only he knew just what hassle and danger they had already had from those people!

While Locky went to have a rest, the Ballygandon Gang decided it was time to start making their plans for the regatta.

"We'll go down to the river," said Molly. "We can practise our fishing."

* * *

From the river-bank, Molly cast her line expertly into the water. Brendan was less skilled, but finally managed to cast *his* line too. Dessy did his best, but could only manage to twirl the line so it came back and wrapped itself round and round his body.

"Good catch!" Brendan laughed. "How shall we cook you, Dessy?"

"Get me out of here!" said Dessy. "I feel like a parcel."

Molly fixed her rod in place and went to disentangle him. Then she handed him a pole with a net on the end and said: "Try this, Dessy. You might catch a few tiddlers."

As Dessy began poking around in the water, he said: "Tiddlers aren't my scene. I'm going to go after a much bigger catch in that lake."

"What sort of catch, Dessy?"

"The Lough Gandon Monster!"

"What's that, Dessy?" said Brendan. "Another of your jokes?"

"No way," said Dessy. "Haven't you heard of it?"

"No, I haven't. Is it the Loch Ness Monster's Irish cousin?"

"*I've* heard of it, all right," said Molly. "There are some legends about it around here. It's supposed to be a giant snakey creature with a head like a dragon, and it lives at the bottom of the lake."

"Has anyone ever seen it?" Brendan wondered.

Molly grinned. "Only after a heavy night at the pub, I reckon."

"A monster! Now that would make a great photograph."

"Perhaps we could make it appear," said Dessy.

"How?" said Brendan. "Will we coat you in sauce, and send you in swimming as bait?"

"You're a hoot, Brendan. I meant we could make, like, a model of it, and get it to pop up out of the lake and frighten the crowds. That way you'd get a grand picture, and who's to know it's not the real thing?"

"Good idea, Dessy," said Molly. "Let's go for it."

"It could make us famous," Brendan declared. "We'll be the Ballygandon Monster Catchers!"

"You never know, it might tempt the real monster up to have a look," said Dessy. "It will think it's a long-lost cousin!"

"I felt a tug at my line!" said Brendan excitedly.

"There you are," Dessy laughed. "The Monster's arrived already!"

"Shut up, Dessy. Brendan's caught something," said Molly. "Here, let me help you." She guided Brendan as he pulled, then let the line go slack, then pulled again. After a few minutes, Molly shouted: "Hey presto!" as Brendan gave

71

a final pull at the line and it came flying up out of the water. On the end of the line a fish wriggled and glinted in the sunlight. It went on wriggling on the bank, till Molly unhooked it and hit its head on a rock.

Dessy winced, then said with false bravado: "Well, it's no monster, but it'll do fine for our tea."

"Catch your own tea, Dessy!" said Brendan.

"Here, I think I've got one too!" said Molly, seizing her rod as the line tugged.

In the end they had four fish to take home with them.

"Well done!" said Molly's mother. "At this rate, you'll be winning the fishing contests at the regatta."

Brendan's father rang to tell them the picture would definitely be in the paper. What was more, there happened also to be a press conference tomorrow morning about the future plans of Jim Shanahan's ministry for the leisure industry. It would be televised, and Brendan's father would be there.

"We can all watch it here together," said Locky.

* * *

Before breakfast, Brendan and Molly were on their bikes, hurrying down to Mrs O'Regan's shop. The picture was there, on the front page, down at the bottom. Standing at the counter, Brendan and Molly both held on to the paper. Mrs O'Regan peered over the counter to see.

"It's dead clear!" said Brendan.

"Yes, Jim Shanahan and Gaby Grantham, you'd recognise them straight away. Great work, Brendan!" Molly slapped him on the back.

Above the photograph in heavy type were the words: **FRIENDS IN HIGH PLACES.** Underneath it on the right, in small print, they saw: *Photograph: Brendan O'Hara.*

"Brendan, you're famous!" said Molly.

"Your name in the paper, eh?" Mrs O'Regan smiled. "There'll be no talking to you, now!"

Molly read out the words beneath the picture:

"Pictured on the new super-boat, the Merry Midas, are its owner, business tycoon Gaby Grantham, and Minister Jim Shanahan, whose department helped to fund the building of the vessel. Could it be that Mr Grantham has decided to pay back some of the funds? Or could there be some other explanation for his handing over this wad of cash? No doubt we will all be informed in due course – or will we?"

"That's putting it up to them all right," said Brendan. "I'll bet there'll be some shenanigans at the press conference tomorrow."

And he was right.

9

Questions for the Minister

While Molly's father looked after the shop, her mother gathered with Locky and the Ballygandon Gang around the television set in the living-room. While they waited for the programme, they admired the picture in the paper. Brendan looked at the byline with his name underneath it, and thought of his possible future career as a photo-journalist. He would win prizes: *News Photographer of the Year: Brendan O'Hara!* He would go to far-off countries and take dramatic pictures of their people and their lifestyle, and they would be published in the news magazines . . .

"Here we go!" said Molly excitedly.

There was a blast of music from the screen, and they saw the words *Meet the Press*. The face of the presenter, Kieran

Darcy, appeared.

"Hello there," he said, "and welcome to *Meet the Press.*"

There was a shot of a room with lines of chairs facing the platform. There were about thirty people in the audience.

"There's Dad!" cried Brendan, pointing at his father who was sitting in the front row.

"And look, in the row just behind him," said Molly. "Isn't that your woman from the boat, the one who was up at the castle?"

"Yes. Lavinia!" Locky exclaimed. "What on earth is she doing there?"

"Keeping an eye on Jim Shanahan, I expect," said Brendan.

"Perhaps she'll ask a question," said Dessy, "like 'What did you do with the money, Jim boy?'"

On the screen, Kieran Darcy was saying: " . . . and meeting our assembled journalists this morning is the Minister for Leisure, Mr Jim Shanahan, TD, unveiling his latest plan for the leisure and tourism industry. Good morning, Minister."

The camera cut to Jim Shanahan. "Good morning, Kieran, it's a pleasure to be here." He smiled at the presenter and then turned to smile directly at the camera.

"He won't be smiling so much when they ask him about your picture, Brendan," said Locky.

"Now, Minister," said Kieran Darcy, "this new plan your department is launching today. . . "

Jim Shanahan began to outline the main points of the plan and how it would help various aspects of the leisure and tourism industry. Charts and graphics came on to the screen to illustrate what he said.

When he had finished, Kieran Darcy asked for questions.

A tall man in a blue suit, with floppy blond hair, stood up. "Minister," he said sharply, "isn't it true that this so-called 'new' plan is simply a re-hash of the usual promises and projections we've heard so often before, and isn't the bottom line that we are paying out more government money and getting less tourists coming into the country?"

"Certainly not, I'm afraid you have your figures wrong once again, George," Jim Shanahan said calmly, with a false smile. "Let me explain . . . "

He produced an elaborate and confusing array of statistics, while other journalists got up to question him on various points. He stayed unruffled and smooth in the face of it all. The Ballygandon Gang were becoming impatient.

"If only they'd let Dad get a word in edgeways!" said Brendan.

"I expect he's biding his time," said Locky. "Yes, here he is now!"

The camera focussed on Brendan's father as he got to his feet and the presenter said: "Pat O'Hara."

"I would like to ask the Minister what explanation he has for this picture which appears on the front page of my own paper this morning." Brendan's father held up the newspaper. The camera zoomed in to show the photograph. "It shows the Minister being given a large sum of money by the businessman Gaby Grantham, owner of the *Merry Midas*, the luxurious new boat which Mr Shanahan's department supplied considerable funds to help to build."

Kieran Darcy turned to Jim Shanahan and said: "Any comment, Minister?"

"Indeed I have a comment!" Jim Shanahan looked flustered. He was frowning angrily. "This picture is typical of the kind of scurrilous gutter journalism in which Mr O'Hara's paper is known to specialise. It is an unauthorised intrusion on a private transaction between Mr Grantham and myself . . . "

"May I ask what kind of transaction?" said Brendan's father, ignoring the insults.

Another voice chimed in, this time a woman journalist: "Yes, Jim, why was he giving you the cash? For some kind of a favour?"

"Like helping to build his boat?" said Brendan's father.

"Certainly not!" Jim Shanahan was getting angrier. "I am under no obligation to disclose what the money was for. As I say, it was a private transaction."

"It's gone a bit public now," said Brendan's father, holding up the paper. There was laughter in the audience.

"Give us an answer," said the woman journalist. "We can always ask Gaby Grantham. Maybe he'd be more frank with us."

Another voice said: "That'll be the day!" There was more laughter.

"All right, all right!" Jim Shanahan said loudly over the hubbub.

"Quiet please!" said Kieran Darcy.

Jim Shanahan leaned forward with a scowl on his face to address the audience. "The reason I didn't disclose the nature of the transaction was this. The money was a gift, for charity. Naturally Mr Grantham wasn't anxious to boast about his goodwill gesture, so he asked me to keep the donation a secret."

"Did you ever hear such a cock-and-bull story?" Locky laughed.

From the mutterings and chuckles they could hear from the audience of journalists, it sounded as if they also had their doubts.

"That was very generous of him," said Brendan's father. "May I ask what charity it was meant for?"

"Well . . . I'm not sure I should disclose . . ." Jim Shanahan faltered.

"I think you *should*, Minister, so that we can all know that everything is above board.."

"Very well . . ." Jim Shanahan's mind seemed to have gone blank, as he desperately tried to think of an answer.

Suddenly a voice from the audience called out: "I can answer that, Minister!" The camera cut to a shot of a woman standing.

"It's Lavinia!" cried Molly.

On the platform, Kieran Darcy was saying: "Can you identify yourself for the audience, please?"

"Certainly," said Lavinia. "Lavinia Longbridge, representing the Boating Chronicle. I am also a colleague of Mr Grantham, who is currently on the high seas, carrying the flag of Ireland and a message of goodwill to distant lands. . . "

"What a load of codswallop!" said Locky.

"I am sure Mr Grantham would be happy for me to identify the charity, since his generous gesture has now been made public knowledge by Mr O'Hara here." She looked towards Brendan's father with a sneery smile. "The charity is one which I am sure will please him. It is the Lough Gandon Regatta, which is being held soon to help protect the fish, birds and other wild creatures of our lakes and waterways. Creatures which as you know are under threat from the environmental pollution which is so . . . "

As she went on, warming to her theme, the Ballygandon Gang looked at one another.

"Not bad, considering she must have thought of it on the spur of the moment," said Locky.

"Well, it's good news for the Regatta and for Ballygandon, anyway," said Molly.

"That's if the money ever gets there!" Brendan was doubtful.

"I think she's trying to get in your father's good books," said Locky, "knowing his family connections with this area and all."

"That won't persuade dad to keep quiet if he finds there's skulduggery going on."

On the screen, Kieran Darcy was looking restless as he listened to Lavinia's continuing waffle about the environment and Gaby Grantham's charitable goodwill. "Thank you very much," he cut in. "I am sure the organisers of the Lough Gandon Regatta will be delighted."

Now Jim Shanahan spoke. "They'll be even more delighted," he said, "when they learn that the *Merry Midas* itself will be sailing up river to Lough Gandon to take part in the festivities!"

"But, Minister – " they heard Lavinia say.

Again Kieran Darcy interrupted her. "Thank you very much, and there I think we can leave the Lough Gandon Regatta for the moment, and get on with some other questions . . . "

The press conference continued. Jim Shanahan gave his answers smoothly. He had recovered his usual confident, smarmy manner.

"He looks relieved to have got out of that corner," said Locky.

"It's very unfair," said Brendan. "He's turned the tables on us. Now people will think he and Gaby Grantham are a pair of saints."

"I doubt it," said Locky, "but it does look as if they've won that round. We'll just have to see what else we can find out about their wheeling and dealing."

"It's a job for the Ballygandon Gang!" said Dessy.

"We should get a chance to investigate when Gaby Grantham is here with the *Merry Midas*," said Molly. "I'm sure Jim Shanahan will be down here as well, after making all that fuss about the regatta."

"I wonder what Lavinia was going to say at the end there," Brendan said. "She looked as if she wasn't too pleased with the Minister's announcement."

"Maybe she didn't know what he was going to say," said Locky. "If we were only there, we might be able to find out more."

"Dad's there. Maybe *he* will."

*   *   *

Indeed, there *was* more to find out. When the programme ended, Brendan's father went out into the foyer of the television studio building with the other journalists.

Lavinia tapped him on the shoulder and said silkily:

"Well, I'm sure you're pleased we cleared up that little question so satisfactorily, Mr O'Hara," she said.

"For the time being," said Brendan's father. Just then Jim Shanahan came by with Kieran Darcy who was thanking him for being on the show.

Lavinia grasped Jim's elbow and said softly: "Minister – can I have a quick word? In private?"

Jim Shanahan said, "What is it?" as she guided him away behind a pillar. Brendan's father hovered at the other side of the pillar, pretending to write in his notebook.

"Why did you say that about the *Merry Midas*?" she hissed.

"It's a great idea," said Jim Shanahan. "Goodwill visit and all that. Should do a lot to raise my profile – and Gaby's."

"But it will mess up his whole schedule!" Lavinia was really annoyed. "You know he's on the way to Europe to collect some very special goods."

"What kind of goods?"

"I'm afraid I can't say."

"Well, he'll just have to get a move on," said Jim Shanahan, "and he can always sail back to visit Lough Gandon instead of coming to Dublin."

"He's going to be furious, believe me."

"I can't help that. He owes me a lot, remember."

"But Jim . . . "

The Minister said loudly: "Thank you, Miss Longbridge, I'll have to go now. Goodbye."

He went across to Kieran Darcy who took him out through the main door to where his ministerial limousine was waiting.

Brendan's father stayed behind the pillar so that Lavinia wouldn't see he'd been eavesdropping. She strode across the foyer and went outside. Through the glass wall of the building he could see her snatch her mobile phone from her bag. He saw her dial and then have an animated conversation, waving her arm in the air. She was probably talking to Gaby Grantham out on 'the high seas' as she had called them. And it did look from her expression as if what she told him had indeed made him furious.

Brendan's father smiled. There was a lot more to be found out about the dealings between Gaby Grantham and Jim Shanahan. And now that the *Merry Midas* was due to sail into Lough Gandon, Brendan's father knew exactly the young people who could help him find it out: the ones who called themselves *The Ballygandon Gang!*

10

Monster Plans

"This is a nice surprise, Pat," said Molly's mother, when Brendan's father arrived at the house in Ballygandon. "We don't see enough of you down here, so we were delighted when you phoned."

"It's business as well as pleasure," said Pat O'Hara. "The paper wants me to cover the Lough Gandon Regatta, and I thought Brendan and Molly and Dessy could show me where it's all going to happen."

"A lot's happening all right," said Brendan. "Sailing and rowing and swimming races, water-skiing, angling competitions . . "

"And maybe even the Lough Gandon Monster will show up," said Dessy.

"Is this one of your jokes, Dessy?"

"Not at all, Mr O'Hara. It's a legend around here, and lots of people have seen it. Well, some have, anyway. It could well turn up when it sees all the juicy human morsels swimming and sailing about for it to devour."

"Well then, I don't think I'll bring my togs after all," Brendan's father laughed. "I don't fancy ending up as dinner for some *Jaws*-type creature."

*   *   *

As he drove them over to Lough Gandon, Brendan's father told them about the conversation he'd overheard between Jim Shanahan and Lavinia.

"I don't think that was part of the plan at all," he said, "Lavinia said Gaby Grantham would be furious at having to bring the boat to Lough Gandon. I think Jim Shanahan thought of it on the spur of the moment, as a way to make himself look good."

"And once he'd announced it, Gaby Grantham has to go along with it," said Molly.

"Exactly. After all, he is supposed to be running the boat partly as a showpiece for the nation, and a charity regatta would be just what it ought to be doing."

"I wonder what was so urgent that he wanted to go straight back to Dublin from his trip," said Brendan.

"That's what you can help me find out," said his father. "When the *Merry Midas* gets here, see what information you can get about just where it's been and what Gaby Grantham has been up to."

"Detective work, eh?" said Dessy. "That's right up our street – or in this case, up our harbour."

* * *

The main harbour on Lough Gandon was at a place called Garrylarkin, which had a small hotel, a pub and a grocery store, as well as a store that supplied fuel and marine equipment for the local boats and the visiting ones too. It had a sturdy harbour wall that jutted out into the lake, as well as a long wooden pier held up by a criss-cross of steel girders. There were two motorboats moored there, while several yachts floated in the harbour. A sleek, handsome yacht was just sailing out of the harbour into the lake. People were fishing from the stone wall.

"I wish I'd brought my fishing rod," said Molly, watching a bearded angler land a brown fish on to the jetty.

They walked up to the end of the pier. "This is where the *Merry Midas* will tie up, I expect," said Brendan.

"Sure is," said a deep voice behind them. They looked round and saw a bulky man with a bushy beard, in a blue fisherman's cap, an Aran sweater and green rubber boots. "It was quite a surprise to hear that that fancy new boat is paying us a visit."

"I think it was a bit of a surprise to Gaby Grantham too," said Molly quietly.

"Captain Corcoran," the man introduced himself. "I run tours and fishing trips around the lake. And I'm the President of the Lough Gandon Regatta."

"The *Merry Midas* should be a big attraction," said Pat O'Hara.

"We'll be keen to see it, that's for sure. It's good to know what they're spending our taxpayers' money on."

"Money well spent, do you think?"

"Squandered, more likely. It would be better used to support the boatmen and the tourist industry in places like this."

"Maybe when you see it, you'll change your mind."

"Maybe, but I doubt it."

Brendan's father explained that he was a journalist writing about the regatta. Captain Corcoran began to give his views about the place and its attractions and how it could flourish much more if people like Minister Jim Shanahan would only get their ideas together.

Brendan and Molly walked along the pier, gazing at the boats and the anglers. Suddenly Brendan looked around and said: "Where's Dessy got to?"

"I thought he was following on behind us," said Molly.

"There's no sign of him," said Brendan. "I hope he hasn't fallen in!"

"We'd have seen him – and heard the splash! I expect he's burrowing around on one of the boats."

Just then they heard Dessy's voice in the distance. "Ahoy there!" he called. "Brendan! Molly! Ahoy there!"

They looked over towards the shore, and saw the figure of Dessy, waving at them with both arms in the air. They walked further down the pier as Dessy ran along the shore to meet them.

"Hi there, shipmates!" he said.

"You're certainly picking up this boating lingo, Dessy," said Molly. "Before long you'll be putting a parrot on your shoulder and singing '*Yo-ho-ho and a bottle of rum!*'."

"Less cheek, Seaman Donovan, or I'll make you walk the plank!"

"You and whose navy?" said Molly, grabbing Dessy and putting an armlock on him, "and less of the Sea*Man,* anyway! I could wrestle you into the harbour, *shipmate!*"

"OK, OK, I give up," said Dessy, and Molly let him go.

"Where did you get to, Dessy?" asked Brendan.

"I was on a search mission. A successful one."

"What are you on about?"

"Just along the shore there, round behind the trees, there's a tiny beach. It's the perfect spot."

"Perfect for what?"

"Launching that terrifying creature of the deep, the Lough Gandon Monster!"

"There *is* no Lough Gandon Monster."

"There will be, when we've finished making it."

Just then they saw Brendan's father coming towards them.

"We won't tell your father just yet, if you don't mind," said Dessy. "We want to surprise everyone."

"There's nothing to tell, anyway," said Brendan.

"There *will* be!" said Dessy.

Brendan's father said he was going to wander around and get some more views from the local people about the regatta and the *Merry Midas.* He'd drive them all back to Ballygandon in an hour's time.

* * *

Dessy led Brendan and Molly along the shore to show them the bay he'd found. They went through the trees on the little headland and found a small cove with a pebbly beach, and a broken-down jetty sticking out into the water.

"Nobody will see us here," said Dessy. "We'll put the monster together and sail it out into the lake. The head will be all luminous so people will see it, and we'll have a tape with roaring monster noises."

"Like when we pretended to be the Phantom Horseman?" said Molly, getting enthusiastic.

"Just like that," said Dessy, "but this time it will be the Phantom Monster."

"It could just work," said Brendan. "Anyway, it'll be fun to give it a go."

"I'm game," said Molly.

"Great," said Dessy. "We can start organising it when we get back to Ballygandon."

* * *

On the drive back, Brendan's father told them that not everyone in Garrylarkin felt the same way as Captain Corcoran about the *Merry Midas*. A lot of them were curious to see it, and pleased that the visit of such a high-profile boat would give the place publicity and bring more tourists there.

"What we need to know is what Gaby Grantham is using the *Merry Midas* for. It clearly wasn't part of his plan to come and be a sight for visitors to gawp at in a place like Lough Gandon."

"And whatever his plan is, does Jim Shanahan know about it?" Brendan wondered.

"That's the big question," said his father. "It would help if we knew exactly where the *Merry Midas* went to, when it left Dublin after that ceremony."

"We'll see what we can do to find out," said Molly.

"My office just rang me when I was going round Garrylarkin," said Brendan's father. "I have to get back to Dublin today for a different story. But I'll be back for the regatta."

*   *   *

When they'd waved Brendan's father off, Dessy said, "Now, it's time for the Monster Plan. Let's start designing."

"I know where we can do that," said Molly. "Let's go down to the library and look for monster legends."

Joan Bright found two or three books that had illustrations of weird creatures from legends and fantasies. There was the sphinx, with a woman's head and a lioness's body, the gryphon which was a cross between a lion and an eagle, Medusa the Gorgon with snakes for hair, who turned anyone who saw her to stone. But best of all, they agreed, was the fire-breathing dragon, like the one slain by Saint George in the legend.

"I wonder how the dragon's head became linked with the Lough Gandon Monster," said Molly, "but it's definitely part of the legend."

"Perhaps Saint George was a swimmer," said Dessy.

"If he was, all that armour he's wearing in the pictures would have weighed him down a bit," said Brendan.

"Anyway, a dragon's head it is!" Dessy hissed at them, pretending to breathe fire. "Now all we've got to do is work out how to make it."

They heard a loud *miaow*. Internet the cat had jumped up on to the table where they had spread the books out.

"We could make it a cat's head instead," said Molly, stroking the cat.

"The Internet," said Brendan. "While we're here, why don't we look it up?"

"For more dragons?" asked Dessy.

"No, for boats. You remember Dad saying it would help to find out where the *Merry Midas* had been? Maybe the Internet would help."

Joan Bright said they were welcome to use the computer room, and after trying various web sites they found a yachting one and keyed in *Merry Midas*. A long catalogue of the names of different boats came on to the screen, in alphabetical order. Alongside each name there was a navigational fix of the boat's whereabouts.

Brendan scrolled down through the list, saying the names as he went: "*Meerkat, Merlin Magic, Mermaid Moll . . . *There it is! *Merry Midas!* That's odd."

"Yes," said Molly, looking over his shoulder. "It says *No Access. Confidential.*"

"It looks as if Gaby Grantham wants to keep his trip a secret," said Dessy.

"It must be recorded somewhere," said Brendan. "The authorities would insist on it."

"Perhaps it's in code," said Molly, "like secret submarine movements."

"We must try and crack it," said Brendan. "But where do we start?"

"This could be the answer," said Dessy, as they watched a jumble of flashing letters come on to the screen.

"Well done, Brendan," said Molly, "you were always the code expert."

"It's not me," said Brendan. "Someone else is giving us a helping hand."

11

Island Secrets

They had got such messages before, when what seemed to be Princess Ethna's spirit floated through cyberspace and infiltrated the library computer. The messages weren't simple: whoever was inventing them seemed to enjoy codes and puzzles. This time, they watched the jumble of letters hurl themselves about the screen with a whizzing sound, until they finally settled into lines they could read:

> One starts jolly
> Two has alighted
> Three's a dolly
> Four begins excited.
> Find the style,
> Find the Isle.

Brendan jotted the words down in his notebook. He gazed at them, baffled, then looked up at the others. Molly shrugged her shoulders. Dessy said: "It beats even my gigantic brain!"

"It's got one-two-three-four," said Brendan. "Maybe they are the four letters of a word, and each line is a clue to one letter."

"Well, *jolly* starts with the letter *J,* so let's try that as the first letter of the word," said Molly.

Brendan wrote it down, then said: "Alighted means come down, like a plane."

"Or a mosquito," said Dessy, making a buzzing noise. "I've got it! A mosquito alights on a dolly, and begins to get excited. Bingo! The code is cracked."

"Or maybe the code-breaker is cracked, in your case," said Molly. "It doesn't make any sense."

"Suppose it's not meant to?" said Brendan. "Suppose Letter Number Two is the first letter again, the *A* of *alighted*" He wrote down an *A* after the *J.*

"In that case Letter Number Three is *D,* the first letter of *dolly.*"

"And Number Four is *E,* beginning *excited.*" Brendan wrote in his notebook and read out: "*J – A – D – E.* That's jade, like the green jewel. My grandmother had a jade necklace."

"What about the rest of it?" Dessy asked. "*Find the style, Find the isle?*"

"Well, we found the style, if that means the code," said Brendan, "and an isle is an island. So the solution could be *Jade Island.*"

93

"Let's get an atlas," said Molly, going out towards the library. Dessy followed.

Brendan turned back and tapped out on the computer the word *Thanks!* The screen flashed on and off, like an acknowledgement. Brendan heard a *miaow* from Internet the cat, who was lying on top of the computer. He stroked her head and said: "And thank you too, Internet!" Then he followed the others into the library.

* * *

"There it is!" cried Molly, pointing at a spot on the map. They had the atlas spread open on one of the tables in the library. They had looked up *Jade Island* in the index and turned to a page which showed Ireland and Wales and the south-west of England. Jade Island was way out in the sea, about halfway between Cornwall and Wexford.

"It looks very isolated," said Brendan. "I wonder why Gaby Grantham would sail the *Merry Midas* there."

"Perhaps he was meeting someone," said Molly.

"I'm sure it wasn't to feed the seagulls," said Dessy. "Hey, do you know what they called the romance between the seagull and the floating sea-marker?"

"I give up, Dessy," said Brendan.

Dessy grinned. "A story of *Gull meets Buoy!*"

"That joke is definitely a walk-the-plank offence!" said Molly.

"We'll have to see what we can find out about the Jade Island trip when the *Merry Midas* arrives in Lough Gandon," Brendan said, "and it's due to arrive tomorrow."

94

"Time to get busy making the Lough Gandon Monster." Dessy screwed up his face and gave a hissing sound, pretending to breathe fire at Brendan.

* * *

Their first call was at Mr Morton's garage, where they examined the pile of old tyres rotting away in his yard. "Well, they're no use to *me*," said the garage owner, when they asked him if he needed them. "You can take a few away if you like. What do you want them for?"

"We're going to float down the river in them," said Brendan.

"You young people have some strange ideas of fun. How will you get them down to the river?"

"We'll roll them!" Dessy declared.

"We've just got to go home first," said Molly, "then we'll come back and get rolling!"

On the way back to Molly's house, Dessy said casually: "Of course, we're going to need an inflatable boat. . . "

"What?" Brendan was startled.

"Well, the Monster's got to float on something – having no body of its own, like."

"I thought we were going to be inside it, floating on the tyres," said Brendan.

"No, the tyres are for the tail of the monster. We cut them in half, and string them together with the curves sticking upwards out of the water in a line, so they look like the humps of the monster's tail, trailing behind."

"And the head is sticking up in front from the inflatable

boat?" Molly asked.

"Exactly," said Dessy, "and behind it we make a body out of draped painted canvas, like a tent, to hide us while we guide the boat."

"You should work in the horror movies, Dessy." Brendan was admiring. "Making *The Creature from the Black Lagoon* would be a doddle for you."

"I'm open to offers," Dessy smiled.

"There's just one problem," said Molly. "Where do we find an inflatable boat?"

They decided to phone Locky as soon as they got back to Molly's house, in case he might have some likely friends or contacts.

"That's a tricky one," Locky said. "My contacts are more in the horse-racing than the aquatic world. But I'll see what I can do. What do you want it for?"

Molly dropped her voice. "You'll keep it a secret, won't you, Grandad?"

"Of course."

Molly explained the plan, and Locky was enthusiastic. "This will put us on the map!" he exclaimed. "That Loch Ness gang will be only trotting after us." He said he would call back that evening.

Molly persuaded her father to lend them a saw, a canvas tarpaulin, and some of the old cardboard boxes the groceries for the shop had come in. They borrowed a roll of wire and some other tools too, and they put them all in a rusting supermarket trolley which was in the yard. They explained that they were making a kind of tent to cover an inflatable boat, as part of the regatta celebrations.

They wheeled the trolley down the road, causing some amusement among people they passed.

"Been doing some shopping?" asked one.

"So *you're* the people doing all this illegal dumping!" said another.

When they reached the garage they collected the tyres. They managed to fit one into the trolley with the other gear, and Brendan said he'd wheel it while Molly and Dessy each rolled a tyre down to the river. They looked a very odd procession as they rolled and racketed along. Once, the trolley hit a bump and started to topple over. Molly and Dessy had to abandon their tyres and rush to steady the load. Along the way they met Mrs O'Rourke who eyed them with suspicion.

"Hello, Mrs O'Rourke," said Molly cheerfully. "We're just doing our bit for the environment, collecting rubbish."

"Well, just don't dump any of it in *my* fields!"

"Oh, we'd never do that," said Molly pleasantly. "Are you going to the regatta?"

"I certainly am," was the answer. "As a matter of fact I have a friend who has invited me on board the most important boat there."

"Oh yes, that will be the *Merry Midas*," said Brendan. "We were on board that in Dublin."

"So I heard," said Mrs O'Rourke, "but this time it will be only VIP's, not riff-raff."

"Proper order!" said Dessy. "Well, jolly good sailing, eh?" He gave a salute and began whistling *The Irish Rover* as they trundled off towards the river.

* * *

"She'll be on board the *Merry Midas* with her friend Lavinia no doubt," said Brendan as they went.

"And the other 'VIPs'," said Dessy. "I say, Brendan me old shipmate, fancy a cocktail on the boat deck?"

"Chin Chin, Dessy, let's splice the mainbrace!" said Brendan.

"What does that mean, for heaven's sake?" asked Molly.

"I've no idea, but they're always saying it in those old naval yarns whenever they have a drink, which seems to be quite often."

"Well, *we'd* better start splicing the monster!"

They wheeled the trolley and rolled the tyres along the river bank to the old boathouse. It was dilapidated and unused now, but there was still a floor and a small jetty there, as well as a broken rowing boat that had sunk to the bottom and was silted up with mud.

"This will make a great monster workshop," said Dessy approvingly, as they unloaded the trolley.

It was hard work sawing the tyres in half and nailing the curved halves to boards so that they would float in the water. They roped the boards together and stood them up in a line along the floor of the boathouse.

"In the water, they'll really look like a snakey monster," said Brendan. He knelt down so that he was level with the floor, and took a photograph. "Look at that!"

He held out the camera so they could look into it and see the picture. The black line of curves could certainly be mistaken for a creature's body, weaving through the surface of the water.

"We can't do much about the main body," said Molly,

"until we get the inflatable boat, and can drape the canvas over it."

"But we can start on the head," said Dessy. He picked up one of the big cardboard boxes and thrust his head into the open end, giving a dragon-style roar. Emerging from the box, he described how they would squash it into a lozenge shape, then stick on a smaller squashed box in front for the nose. "We'll get some bunches of feathers for the ears, and then paint it in really bright colours, with great big fierce eyes, and some white pointed sticks in the mouth for fangs."

They set to work with the cardboard and heavy sticky tape, and it wasn't long before they had something that did have the look of an animal's head, even if it was chunky and angular like a modern sculpture. They slapped on the paint, and drew the gigantic eyes, and stuck on the feathers and fangs. Brendan took another photograph and showed it to them.

"That looks fantastic!" said Dessy. "It will be on the front page: *LOUGH GANDON MONSTER, THE TERROR OF THE DEEP!*"

"I'm just wondering," said Brendan, "how we're going to get the Lough Gandon Monster from here to Lough Gandon?"

"We can pack it in pieces into Locky's car," said Molly, "and we can inflate the boat and put it all together when we get to the little beach Dessy found."

"Assuming Locky has managed to find a boat," said Brendan.

They were in luck. Locky telephoned that evening to say that his friend Oliver at Horseshoe House had a nephew who used to do some fishing, and had an old inflatable boat in his garage. Locky could collect it on the way to Ballygandon the next day.

"See you tomorrow about eleven," said Locky. "Long live the inflatable monster!"

* * *

Next morning they decided to go to the library again to see what more they could find out about Jade Island. Joan Bright found them some books about marine history.

"It seems to have been uninhabited for a hundred years or more," said Molly. "Before that, there were some fishermen who built sheds for shelter and stayed there for a while. It sounds like a wild place."

"Here's something else," said Brendan, looking at another book. "It says: *Jade Island was so far off the beaten track, it made an ideal place for smugglers and pirates to hide themselves, and their stolen treasure*"

"Treasure?" Molly wondered. "Could that be why Gaby Grantham went there?"

"We'll start trying to find out," said Brendan, "when the *Merry Midas* sails into Lough Gandon today."

12

A Champagne Welcome

For the moment, the most important boat for the Ballygandon Gang was not the *Merry Midas*, but the inflatable boat that Locky was going to bring them. They crowded round his old car when it rattled into the yard outside the Donovans' grocery store.

"Mission accomplished!" said Locky, stepping out of the car. "Have a look in the boot."

Brendan opened the boot and they saw a great pile of grey rubber material, all folded and squashed together. Brendan started to pull it out, but Locky said: "Don't take it out here, Brendan. It was hard enough to squash it all in. Once it's out, we may never get it back in again."

"Let's drive it straight down to the boathouse," said

Dessy. "We can inflate it there."

"Then how would we get it over to Lough Gandon?" asked Molly. "We can't float it along the roads."

"Good point," said Locky. "I'd better drive it straight over to Lough Gandon and we'll inflate it there."

"What about the other parts of the monster?" Dessy asked. "We're going to have to get them over to the lake as well, and put them all together on the spot."

"They'll fit in the back of the car, won't they?" said Locky.

"With any luck," said Brendan.

"Then let's start packing!" They all got into the car and Locky drove towards the river.

*   *   *

"We'll have to park here," said Molly, as they reached a gate that led from the road on to the towpath, "and bring all the stuff from the boathouse along to the car."

It took them a couple of trips to and fro to carry the tyres and the canvas and the boxes and tools along beside the river to the gate. They packed them into the car.

"There's only one problem," said Brendan. "Now there's no room for any passengers."

"We could squeeze one of you in," said Locky, "but that's about it. Unless you like to ride on the roof."

"Like on the buses," said Dessy. "Move along there, plenty of room upstairs!"

"I don't fancy it," said Brendan. "Dessy, you're the smallest. Why don't you squeeze in among the gear, and show Locky where your little beach is? Molly and I can bike over to Lough Gandon. It will only take half an hour or so."

"OK," said Dessy. "Well, Locky, let's get this monster on the move."

"I hope you're not referring to my car," said Locky, climbing into the driver's seat.

* * *

As Molly and Brendan stopped at the top of the hill and looked down ahead of them, Lough Gandon was spread out before them, with trees lining the shores. They could see the houses and the harbour of Garrylarkin. There were striped marquees set up on the road beside the lake, and flags flying to celebrate the regatta. Sailing boats and rowing boats pottered about on the water.

A motor-boat towing a water-skier behind it sliced the surface of the lake, breaking the peaceful air with its roar. Then the roar stopped as the boat came to a halt. The skier had fallen off.

"Look over there," said Molly, pointing. In the distance, where the big river entered the lake, they could see a large gleaming white boat, with the sunlight reflecting on its glass windows.

"The *Merry Midas*!" said Brendan.

"All the way from Jade Island," said Molly.

"I wondered if Gaby Grantham was going to turn up," said Brendan. "According to what my father heard, he wasn't too pleased with Jim Shanahan saying he had to come here."

"I suppose we'll be seeing Jim Shanahan himself at the

opening of the regatta tomorrow."

"Yes, and maybe we can get more of the lowdown on the deals between him and Gaby."

"Meanwhile, on with the monster-making," said Molly. "Let's hope Locky and Dessy have the boat inflated by now."

*   *   *

But inflating the boat had proved more of a problem than they had expected. They had laid the flat rubber canvas of the boat out on the small pebble beach. Locky worked the pump while Dessy held on to the rubber sections of the dinghy, making sure the nozzle of the pump stayed pressed on to the air vent. Sometimes he'd relax his grip, and the nozzle sprang away with a hiss of escaping air.

"I think I'll buy myself a motor cruiser next time," said Locky.

They had just got the whole boat inflated when Brendan and Molly arrived.

"Hey, you look relaxed enough, Dessy," said Brendan, looking at Dessy who was lying spread out in the bottom of the boat.

"Don't you believe it," said Dessy. "We boat-builders have been working hard."

"He's right," said Locky. "Now show us how we put all this clobber together." He indicated the piles of canvas and painted boxes and wooden poles and coils of wire which were lying under the trees which shielded the little beach.

"I think we should try out the boat first," said Brendan. "We can sail it out into the lake towards the harbour over there, and watch the *Merry Midas* arriving."

"Great idea," said Dessy. "Welcome aboard!"

"You're going to have to get out first," said Molly. "I'm not going to try and push this into the water with you lounging in it."

Reluctantly Dessy climbed out, and the three of them bent down and began to push the boat along the pebbles to the water's edge.

"It's floating," said Locky.

"It's floating away!" cried Dessy. "Grab hold of it!" He lunged towards the boat with his feet in the water, and flung himself into it.

"Well done, Dessy!" Molly applauded.

"It's still floating away!" said Dessy. "I'm drifting. Throw me a paddle, quick!"

"I saw one somewhere," said Locky, "when we were unpacking . . . " He began to rummage among the piles of gear.

"Here's a rope," said Brendan, picking up the end of a long piece of rope that was strewn near the pile. He flung it towards the floating dinghy. Dessy made a grab and caught it.

"Hold on, Dessy!" said Brendan, as he grasped his end of the rope and began to pull. Gradually the boat came to a stop, and then as Brendan went on pulling it floated back to the edge of the beach.

"You nearly had me cast adrift in the middle of the lake," said Dessy. "The shipwrecked sailor of Lough Gandon."

"Well, you've proved the boat floats all right," said Molly.

"Here, I've found a paddle," said Locky, holding up a

short wooden oar.

"Here's another one," said Brendan. "We should be able to steer with those."

"Then away we go," said Dessy. "Climb aboard before I drift off again." Brendan and Molly scrambled in to join him. It was a tight squeeze. They looked over at Locky.

"I'll sit this one out," he said. "I'm a good deal heavier than you lot, anyway. I'll stay here and keep an eye on your stuff. I'll be the sentry on the shore."

"Thanks, Locky," said Brendan. "We won't be long." He sat at the front end while Molly and Dessy put a paddle in the water each side. The boat sailed slowly out into the lake.

"Look, the *Merry Midas* is in the harbour," said Molly. They stopped paddling and looked across the water.

The big boat gave a hoot of its horn as it came alongside the pier. Through the girders that held the wooden pier up they could see the bottom part of the *Merry Midas*, while the open upper deck was level with it. The man called Larry had stepped on to the pier and was tying up the boat to a metal post. Gaby Grantham in his blazer and naval-style cap stepped off the deck on to the pier. They could see some of the local people greeting him, led by Captain Corcoran. Lavinia was there shaking hands as well. Larry hovered in the background, but no one greeted him. Eventually he went back on to the boat and they saw him go below down the stairs.

Captain Corcoran was pointing along the pier towards the shore, where there were some trestle tables set up with white cloths on them. There were champagne bottles and glasses on the tables.

106

Captain Corcoran led the way, while Gaby Grantham and Lavinia and the other greeters followed.

"Let's paddle over there and take a closer look," said Brendan.

"What if they see us?" asked Dessy.

"They won't notice us," said Molly, "and anyway they're too busy just now guzzling champagne. We can paddle across and sneak our boat in among the girders under the pier. They'll never spot us there."

There were other small boats on the lake, some with people fishing from them. There was a raft too, where two or three sunbathers were lying. One got up and dived into the water and began swimming around. But nobody paid any heed to their boat. They were just another craft floating along.

*   *   *

As they sailed towards the pier, Dessy said: "We haven't got a name."

"I always said you were forgetful," said Molly. "Your name's Dessy, remember?"

"You're a scream, Molly. I mean our boat hasn't got a name. We should call it something."

"How about the *Merry Monster?*" Brendan suggested.

"Good thinking," said Dessy, "the *Merry Monster* it is! Perhaps we can borrow some of their champagne and have a proper launching."

"I think we'll save the celebrations till later," said Brendan, "when we've found out what Gaby is up to."

They nudged the boat in among the girders underneath the wooden pier. Now they were right next to the side of the *Merry Midas.*

"If I stood up," said Brendan, "I could even look in at that porthole."

"You'll rock the boat and land us all in the drink," said Dessy.

"Wait," said Molly. "Dessy, if you and I steady the boat by holding on to these girders, and Brendan leans on the side of the *Midas,* it just might work."

She and Dessy each gripped one of the sloping girders, and Brendan stood up carefully. He began to wobble a bit, then he steadied himself by spreading out his hands on the side of the big boat. Now the porthole was level with his face.

"Hey, it's a little bit open," he said softly. "I can see in. It's that stateroom as they called it, down below decks. There's no one there."

"They're all ashore, boozing," said Dessy.

Just then there was a shrill ringing tone. It was coming from somewhere in the state room. Brendan ducked, as he saw the man called Larry moving across the room. He could hear Larry say: "Yes?" and then, "Who wants to speak to him?" There was a pause and then Larry said: "OK, Minister, I'll get him for you. Hold on."

A few moments later, they heard Larry's feet as he stepped off the *Merry Midas* and on to the pier. Looking up, they could see him through the gaps in the wooden slats above them. He moved off down the pier, and soon afterwards came back again. Gaby Grantham was with him.

"What does that pestering fellow want?" he said, stepping on to the boat.

"He didn't say," said Larry, "but he sounded grumpy."

"What else is new?"

Peering through the porthole, with his head to one side so he couldn't be seen, Brendan looked into the stateroom. He heard Gaby Grantham come down the stairs, then saw him go across the room and pick up a portable phone that was lying on the table.

"Yes, Jim, what is it?" he said sharply. "I've only just got here." There was a pause, then Gaby Grantham said: "Yes, I *know* you're coming down here tomorrow – aren't you playing the Big Cheese and declaring the whole shebang open and all that? Why did you have to summon me way out to this backwater as well? . . . OK, OK, it was to cover your tracks with that photograph. Charity, you said the money was for? That's a laugh. It's lining your pockets as we speak."

There was a pause while Gaby Grantham listened. He was pacing up and down. Brendan ducked down in case he looked his way. Then he heard Gaby explode with fury.

"You want *more?* You're one greedy politician all right, Jim. How much? . . . *What?!* . . . Well, let's wait till you get here, shall we, and then we'll see." There was another pause, then Gaby said: "No, that prowling lot with the camera will *not* be here! We've seen to that. Goodbye, Jim."

Brendan grinned. He knelt down in the boat to tell the others what he had heard. Then they heard footsteps above them on the pier. Looking up, they saw it was Lavinia. She boarded the boat.

Brendan stood up again and peered through the porthole.

"Trouble?" said Lavinia as she came down the stairs into the state room.

"Only Slick Jim, asking for more. He's as bad as Oliver Twist, that bloke."

"What will you do?"

"Oh, pay him off. What we give him is chicken-feed compared with what we've now got on board."

Brendan saw him slide open a concealed panel in the wall. He took out a small red box and he and Lavinia gazed at it.

"Hidden treasure," she said.

"Hidden from everyone," said Gaby Grantham, "except you and me." They both smiled.

13

The Hidden Treasure

B rendan watched as Gaby Grantham opened the lid of the box and took something out. He held it up between his thumb and forefinger. It glinted in the light.

Gaby and Lavinia stared at it.

"Worth a trip to Jade Island, weren't they?" said Gaby.

"And worth a lot more than jade," said Lavinia.

Gaby picked up the box and rattled it. "The sound of a fortune," he said. "We'd have offloaded them by now if that idiot Jim Shanahan hadn't made us come here first."

"When will you sail back to Dublin?"

"Just as soon as Jim has done his speechifying and glad-handing at the opening ceremony," said Gaby. "Then it's up with the anchor, and off we go!"

111

He put the gleaming object back in the box and closed it. Then he put the box back in the cupboard and slid the panel closed.

"But while we wait," he said, "we might as well enjoy these culchies' hospitality." He moved away towards the stairs leading to the upper deck.

"I'll be right after you," said Lavina. "Just got to do the face up a bit."

"See you soon then," said Gaby, going up the stairs. Brendan crouched down as Gaby Grantham stepped off the boat and moved away along the pier.

Brendan whispered quickly to the others about the red box and the gleaming thing which Gaby had taken from it.

"What do you think it was?" asked Dessy.

"I don't know, but there were more in the box, and they seem to be worth a lot."

"Could it be diamonds?" Molly wondered. She stood up in the boat and looked through the porthole.

"We'd better get back to Locky," said Brendan.

Molly turned to them and put her finger to her lips. "Just a moment," she whispered. "I'm watching Lavinia."

Molly peered through the porthole. She saw Lavinia open her handbag, but it wasn't make-up she took out. It was a small red box. She glanced around furtively, then leaned over and slid open the wooden panel in the wall. She reached in and took out the other box, just like the one from her handbag. Then she put her own box into the cupboard and slid the panel shut. She put the other box on the table and opened it. She reached in her hand and scooped something up. She held it in the palm of her hand and gazed at it.

Then she tilted her hand over the box. Molly saw a trickle of bright glassy objects fall back into the box. They *must* be diamonds, thought Molly, as she saw Lavinia close the box and put it in her handbag. She moved towards the stairs.

Molly crouched down and whispered: "She's coming out." They heard the clatter of Lavinia's shoes on the pier as she walked off to join the party on the shore.

"OK, let's get back to base," she said.

*   *   *

As they paddled back to the beach, Molly told the others what she had seen.

"It looks like she plans to doublecross Gaby and keep the diamonds for herself," said Brendan.

"So what's in the other box?" Dessy wondered.

"I don't know, but they looked exactly alike. She probably hopes Gaby won't open the fake box until she's got away."

"She won't want to rouse his suspicions yet," said Molly. "My guess is, she'll let him sail off without her after the ceremony tomorrow, and do a disappearing act then."

"What will she do with the diamonds in the meantime?" asked Dessy. "She'll have to hide them somewhere."

"Hey, look at that!" cried Brendan, pointing back towards the shore. They saw Lavinia leave the champagne-drinking group, walk casually along the road and get into a car. As the car drove off, Molly said: "I know that car. It's Mrs O'Rourke's!"

"We've got to see where they go," said Brendan. "Paddle like mad!"

They nudged the boat on to the beach in the little bay where Locky was waiting.

"Locky, we've no time to lose," said Molly. "We must take your car right now. Come on."

They hastily hid the boat and the gear among the trees and put the canvas over it, Then they got into Locky's car.

They asked him to drive up towards the main road where they'd seen Mrs O'Rourke's car heading. They were in luck. When they reached the main road, they could see her in the distance. Locky followed.

"She's heading back towards Ballygandon," he said.

"We'll just have to follow them," said Brendan.

When Mrs O'Rourke's car reached Ballygandon, she drove down the main road past Molly's parents' store. Then they saw the car turn off on to the little road that led to the hill and the castle. Keeping his distance, Locky followed. They saw Mrs O'Rourke's car stop where the road ended. Locky stopped too, far enough away not to be noticed. They watched Mrs O'Rourke and Lavinia get out of the car and start climbing the rocky path towards the castle.

"That must be where they're going to hide the box," said Locky.

"We can't follow them up there or they'll see us," said Brendan.

"Let's come back later and search," said Molly. "When we find the hiding place, we can tip off the guards."

"I don't think we should do that just yet," said Brendan. "There's nothing to connect Lavinia or Gaby Grantham with the box. They could just deny that they know anything about it."

"They might even claim *we* stole it," said Dessy. "After all, I could easily be mistaken for that well-known smuggler, *Daredevil Diamond Dessy!*"

"Once we know just where it is," said Molly, "we can set a trap for Lavinia and Mrs O'Rourke."

"And when Gaby Grantham finds out he's been double-crossed," said Brendan, "it won't only be the guards who are after that pair!"

"We'll come back and search when the coast is clear," said Molly. "Meanwhile we can go and wait at home."

* * *

They were having a meal at the Donovans' house when Brendan's father arrived. He was preparing to cover the opening of the regatta the next day, and hoping to find out more about the dealings between Jim Shanahan and Gaby Grantham.

They told him what they had overheard Gaby tell Lavinia about paying off Jim Shanahan, and said they suspected Gaby was involved in smuggling too. They didn't want to say anything about the boxes until they had found the hiding place and exposed the plot.

"It sounds as if Gaby Grantham's activities are even murkier than we thought," said Brendan's father. "There could be a really big story here. And this time we won't let Jim Shanahan get away with claiming he's doing it all for charity."

Later the Ballygandon Gang said they would take Molly's dog Tina out for a walk. They made their way towards the castle and climbed the hill. It was beginning to get dark, and the crows were wheeling around in the grey sky, getting ready to settle in their trees for the night. Their cawing cries sounded mournful as they soared above the silhouetted ruins of the castle.

They clambered over the crumbled stones of the outer wall, and looked around. The arches and the walls and the old tower stood silent.

"They could have hidden it anywhere," said Brendan.

"Listen," Molly whispered. There seemed to be a faint sighing sound, or was it the wind? It grew louder.

"I think it's coming from Princess Ethna's Tower," Brendan said. They crossed the courtyard to where an arch opened on to the tower stairway. They looked up the stairs. Somewhere up in the tower they could see a faint purple glow. Molly began to creep up the stairs, leading Tina behind her. Then she heard the dog give a whimpering sound. Tina stopped and wouldn't move any further. She went on whimpering. Suddenly, from further up the stairs, there was another sound: a ferocious growling and barking. Molly looked up. At the top of the stairs she saw the snarling face of another dog. It bared its fangs at her. Molly recognised Lonnigan, the big fierce hound that belonged to Seamus Gallagher, the owner of a pub in nearby Killbreen. He had sometimes been involved with Mrs O'Rourke in various crooked schemes which the Ballygandon Gang had been able to foil. Mrs O'Rourke must have borrowed him from Seamus to guard the hiding place of the box of diamonds.

"It's Lonnigan!" Molly called down to Brendan and

Dessy. She looked up and saw the purple glow get brighter on the stairway behind the snarling dog. Lonnigan was tied by a lead to a metal ring in the wall of the stairway, which at one time must have held a rope that acted as a banister.

Seeing Tina down below him, Lonnigan was in a rage to leap down and attack her.

"Shut up, Lonnigan!" cried Molly, as Tina began to bark back at the huge dog. Lonnigan gave another lunge forwards, and the lead broke. He dashed past Molly, nearly toppling her over, and leaped at Tina. Molly knew her own dog, brave as she was, was no match for Seamus's bruiser.

"Run, Tina!" she cried, letting go of Tina's lead. Tina ran down the stairs and into the courtyard, and Lonnigan followed. But Tina wasn't going to flee from the big bully. She turned and snapped back at him. Lonnigan seized her by the scruff of her neck and held on. Tina writhed and wriggled but couldn't get away.

"He'll kill her!" cried Molly, running across and trying to pull Lonnigan away. Brendan and Molly joined in, and soon the three of them as well as the dogs were tumbling and wrestling in the courtyard.

Suddenly they heard a shrill, high-pitched sound that pierced their ears. It got higher and higher until they couldn't hear it any more: but the dogs still could. They screwed up their faces in pain.

They were both shivering. Molly knew that once again the spirit of Ethna was trying to help: she clasped her hands over Tina's ears to muffle the sound, but clearly Lonnigan could still hear it. The big dog began to whimper, then to run around in circles. Finally it streaked away through an arch-

117

way, ran towards the outer wall, and jumped over it and fled down the hill.

Tina stopped shaking. Molly took her hands away from Tina's ears, and the dog licked her face.

The three of them picked themselves up. They looked towards the tower. They could still see the faint purple glow up at the top of the stairs. This time Brendan went up the stairs towards it. The others followed. Brendan reached the point where the broken stairs stopped. He looked over the edge to the castle floor far below. He saw that the glow was coming from a gap in the wall, near the metal ring. He reached in and felt around. He could feel something there. He grasped it and drew out his hand. There was the red box.

He brought it down the stairs and they all gathered round as carefully he opened the lid. Inside was a little pile of bright objects like the one he had seen Gaby hold up. They each took one and held it up gingerly. They all agreed that they would have thought these were just pieces of glass, but Gaby had called them 'hidden treasure'. They must indeed be diamonds.

"I wonder what's in the box Lavinia put in, instead of this one," said Dessy.

"Not what Gaby expects, that's for sure," said Molly.

They put the diamonds back in the box and Brendan went up the stairs with it. He placed it in the hole in the wall once more. He saw the purple glow inside fade away.

As they made their way in the gathering dark along the stony path down the hill, Molly said: "We'll have to keep our eye on Lavinia tomorrow, so she doesn't go and dash off with the loot."

Brendan said: "My guess is she'll hang around the *Merry Midas* till Gaby's ready to leave, so he doesn't get suspicious."

* * *

When they all joined the crowds on the shore near the pier next day, Lavinia was indeed with Gaby on the deck of the *Merry Midas.* They smiled and chatted with the people who came along the pier to admire the boat, but they didn't invite anyone on board.

"I suppose they're going to wait to greet Jim Shanahan when he arrives," said Brendan.

At that moment they heard the roar of motor cycles approaching along the road. They came into view, and behind them again came the ministerial limousine. It came to a halt, and the Minister stepped out, waving to the crowds. There was some applause and the odd cheer, and someone called out: "Hiya, Jim!"

The Minister was brought into a marquee, where tables and drinks had been laid out for a reception. Brendan's father and other journalists went inside with the group of VIP's. Peering through a gap in the marquee, Brendan, Molly and Dessy could see Jim Shanahan shaking hands and chatting. He seemed to be looking around for someone.

There was a call for silence, then a man in a blazer said: "Now, ladies and gentlemen, if you have all refreshed yourselves, it is time to call on the Minister to declare the Lough Gandon regatta open. Would you all accompany us outside, please?"

Outside the marquee near the entrance to the pier there was a platform with chairs and a table and a microphone on it. The Minister was ushered to the chair in the middle. He was still looking round among the crowds. Then he smiled. Coming forward from the pier was Gaby Grantham, carrying a book. He stepped on to the platform and shook hands with Jim Shanahan.

"Good day, Minister," he said. "I've got that material you wanted."

"Oh, good, good," said Jim Shanahan rather nervously.

"It's all here, in this album," said Gaby, opening it. Jim Shanahan muttered: "Later, perhaps."

"Oh no, you must see it now. It's photographs of the good ship *Merry Midas,* which you did so much to help to build."

"Oh, delightful," said Jim Shanahan, beginning to leaf through the album.

"You'll particularly like the items at the end," said Gaby. Jim Shanahan opened the final cover of the album, looked at it, and closed it again quickly.

"Thank you," he said.

Brendan was standing behind the platform, and could just see the album he was holding. He was sure he saw, just before the Minister snapped it shut, that the last page of the album was a transparent folder, crammed with banknotes.

14

The Monster Sets Sail

This was the evidence they needed, thought Brendan. If only he could get a close-up look at the album, and even take a photograph. His wish was granted in an unexpected way. Jim Shanahan had taken a sheaf of notes for his speech out of his pocket, so he needed his hands to hold them. He had looked around for somewhere to put the album, and laid it down on a small table beside his chair.

"Ladies and gentlemen, it is with great pleasure that I come here today . . ." The Minister began his speech, while Brendan and Molly and Dessy crouched down behind the platform.

Molly was holding Tina, hoping she wouldn't interrupt

the speech with any barking – though Molly thought a bark from Tina would have more interest than listening to Jim Shanahan droning on. She had relaxed her grip on Tina's lead. Unfortunately, the dog saw a bee buzzing around just above her head. With a yelp, she leaped at it, breaking free from Molly's hold. The bee landed on the album lying on the table. Tina grabbed the album in her jaws and shook it. Then she jumped down and ran into the space underneath the platform.

There were cries of "What's going on?" and "Grab that dog!" as the Minister stopped in mid-speech.

"Come here, Tina!" cried Molly, as she and Brendan crawled under the platform after Tina. The dog was shaking the album and growling, as if it was some kind of prey. Molly grasped her by the collar. Brendan snatched the album from her jaws. This was his chance! Quickly he spread it out on the ground and photographed it, then opened it at the first page and took another picture. Finally he opened it at the last page where the folder of banknotes could be seen, and took a picture of that.

"Got it!" he said triumphantly. They crawled back out, and saw that people including the Minister were hunting around under the table for the album.

"Here it is," said Molly, handing it up to Jim Shanahan.

"You'll find it's all there," said Brendan, and Molly added: "There's no damage – just a few tooth-marks!"

Jim Shanahan snatched the album and glared at them. He wasn't the only one. Gaby and Lavinia were both looking angrily over the back of the platform.

"It's *them!*" hissed Lavinia. "Those dreadful kids who

122

were at the launch in Dublin. Get after them, Larry." The check-suited man appeared from behind her, and jumped down behind the platform. But Tina, growling, sank her jaws into his trouser leg and held on.

"Get off. Get off me!" shouted Larry, flapping his hand at her.

Brendan, Molly and Dessy dodged through the flap into the marquee, and rushed across and out the other side. "We'll run for the beach!" Molly cried as they dodged and weaved through the crowd. Tina let go of Larry and was speeding behind them. Larry was clutching his leg and limping after them, but they were too fast for him, and he soon gave up. Before long they had reached the little beach where Locky was waiting for them.

"Been running races?" he asked, as they all sat down on the ground to get their breath back.

"Escaping, more like," said Brendan. "With the evidence!" He passed round the camera so they could look into it and see his pictures of the album and the money tucked inside it.

"They'll be after us again," said Locky. "That camera is deadly." They remembered the previous chase and the determination of their pursuers.

"Where shall we go?" Locky wondered. "I don't fancy hiding out again in that hole in the wall at the castle."

"I know!" cried Dessy. "Let's launch the monster!"

"Great idea!" said Molly. "It's a perfect hiding-place. They'll never know it's us."

Quickly they draped the canvas over the struts in the boat. It was bright green and painted to look like a dragon's

123

scales. They attached the head to a tall pole at the front. Then they put the curvy tail on the back. They pushed the boat to the water's edge, and when it started to float, Molly and Dessy jumped in.

"Hold it there!" said Brendan, going a few steps along the beach and holding up his camera.

He took a couple of pictures, then joined them on the boat. He and Molly seized a paddle each.

"Locky, remember to switch on the sound effects when we are out on the lake."

"Aye aye, Captain!" said Locky, holding up the tape recorder.

As they paddled out into the lake, Locky moved along the bank, keeping level with them. On the far shore, they could see the pier and the *Merry Midas* and the other boats. The platform ceremony seemed to be still going on. Then they heard applause, and they could see Jim Shanahan shaking hands with all the VIP's. He had the album clutched firmly in his left hand.

They saw Gaby Grantham shake hands with him too, then stride up the pier towards where the *Merry Midas* was moored, followed by Lavinia, with Larry limping behind them.

"He was planning to sail after the ceremony, wasn't he?" asked Brendan.

"Yes, with what he thinks is a box of real diamonds," said Molly. "Should we alert the guards now? We want to stop him sailing so he can be caught."

"I'm not sure the guards would believe us," said Brendan, "and anyway, with the Minister there he could probably bluff it out."

"Let's create a distraction," said Dessy. "Time for the appearance of the Lough Gandon Monster!"

They paddled further out into the lake, then signalled to Locky on the shore. Locky gave a thumbs-up sign, and held up the tape recorder. He flicked a switch. A series of loud roars went booming across the water. They saw the crowd on the shore looking towards them, and pointing. On the deck of the *Merry Midas* they could see Gaby and Lavinia gazing out at them. Larry was at the stern of the boat, casting off the rope.

"They're sailing out," said Brendan.

"But what about Lavinia?" said Molly. "She's still on board. She surely wouldn't leave the real diamonds behind?"

Just then they saw Gaby go up to the bridge of the boat and take the steering wheel, looking out ahead. Larry stowed the rope and came up to join him. As they watched, Lavinia hurried to the stern and jumped the widening gap between the boat and the pier. She hurried off down the pier and into the crowds, without Gaby noticing she had abandoned ship.

The engines of the *Merry Midas* revved up as it began to turn to face towards the far end of the lake, where it could get out into the river and eventually out to sea.

Suddenly their own boat began to rock from side to side. "What's happening?" cried Brendan. "Hold on to the sides."

"Grab the pole at the front," said Molly. "The head's wobbling about."

The boat continued to rock as the unexpected waves hit it.

"Wow!" shouted Dessy, "I think we've done it!"

"What, Dessy?"

"We've disturbed the real Lough Gandon Monster! It's coming up to attack us!"

"No, it can't be!" said Brendan – but he didn't sound too sure.

"I know what it is," said Molly. "Look at the *Merry Midas*. It's turning around, and making a wake at the stern. The ripples are hitting our boat."

"Ripples? They're more like waves!" said Dessy. But they could see Molly was right. He didn't know whether to be relieved or disappointed.

The inflatable boat was rocking more and more, as the roaring went on from Locky's tapes on the shore. The crowd near the pier cheered as they saw the strange floating creature bob up and down and tilt from side to side.

"Hold her steady!" cried Dessy, standing up and trying to hold the head of the monster, which was in danger of coming right off. He seized the metal pole which the head was attached to and leaned on it. Then to his alarm he saw that the end of the pole had gone through the bottom of the boat. Dessy held on to the monster's head, while he watched water begin to seep through the tear in the rubber floor. The pole had disappeared through it and sunk into the lake.

Brendan pulled down the draped canvas and tried to stuff it into the hole, but he only succeeded in making it bigger. Now water was lapping around their feet.

"We must paddle for base before she sinks!" said Molly. She and Brendan began to paddle furiously. The boat rocked from side to side. Dessy was still trying to hold the monster's head up in the air, but as the rocking went on he lost his balance. There was a splash as he fell into the lake.

"Dessy, grab the paddle!" said Brendan, holding it out.

"It's all right. I'll swim," Dessy shouted. "The boat will be lighter now. You paddle on!"

"Are you OK?" cried Locky from the bank. "I'll go and get help."

"We're fine," called Brendan. "We're going back to the beach." He looked around. Dessy was several metres away from them now, and a current seemed to be carrying him further. Not far beyond him was the stern of the *Merry Midas*. Dessy made up his mind.

"I'll go that way!" he called, and began to swim.

"Dessy, come back!" shouted Molly, as she and Brendan watched him swimming towards the big boat.

"We must keep paddling," said Brendan. "We're sinking fast." As they paddled they looked across the lake and saw Dessy reach the side of the *Merry Midas*. There was a metal ladder on the side of the boat, and Dessy grabbed it and began to climb up. He looked back at them and gave a wave, then the thumbs-up sign. They saw him reach the top of the ladder. Then they saw a hand grab hold of him and drag him on board.

15

Horror at the Tower

Brendan and Molly got the boat to the pebbly beach, to be welcomed by Locky and Tina. The dog jumped up and down gleefully, barking and licking Molly's face.

"They've kidnapped Dessy!" said Brendan. "We must tell the guards right away."

"Into the car!" said Locky.

They all piled in and he drove round the shore to the end of the pier. Brendan saw Emma Delaney, the guard from Ballygandon. He jumped out of the car and ran over to her. Seeing them talking, Brendan's father came over, and Molly and Locky joined them too. They were all talking at once, trying to explain about the diamonds and the switching of boxes and Gaby Grantham and the Minister and the Lough

Gandon Monster and Dessy's swim to the boat.

"Hold on. Hold on," said Emma, as another guard came over to them, asking what was going on. "They all seem to be panicking about monsters and ministers and diamonds and Dessy . . ."

"It's Dessy we've got to worry about," said Brendan. "He's been kidnapped. He's out there, on the *Merry Midas,* and it's sailing away. He could be in real danger."

"We'll tell the boat to stop," said the second guard. "The megaphone's here in the car."

He reached into the police car nearby and took out the cone-shaped megaphone. Emma took it and ran a little way up the pier. She put it to her mouth and shouted: *"Ahoy there! Merry Midas! This is the guards. We want you to return with your passenger."*

They saw Gaby Grantham on the bridge, picking up his own megaphone. *"No can do!"* he called. *"We are leaving now. Passenger safe. We'll drop him off later. Goodbye!"*

"Drop him off?" said Brendan. "He might be going to drop him literally – in the water!"

"We'll commandeer a motor launch," said Emma, "and get after them."

* * *

On board the *Merry Midas,* Dessy was sitting on the deck, his hands tied to a railing. There was a piece of rope in his mouth, pulled tight and tied at the back of his head. It was a gag to prevent him shouting for help. Larry was sitting on a nearby bench, watching him.

"Don't do anything stupid, and you'll be all right," said Larry.

Through the gag, Dessy tried to say: "Tell Gaby. Look at diamonds. Diamonds gone!" It all came out as a jumble of words, but Larry decided to call Gaby Grantham.

"Boss! You'd better come here!"

"What's the problem?" Gaby called. He handed over the steering wheel to one of the crew, and came down to the deck.

"He's saying something about diamonds," said Larry.

Gaby Grantham looked alarmed. "Diamonds? What does he know about diamonds?"

"Search me, boss. I don't know what he's on about."

Dessy realised that Larry probably *didn't* know exactly what cargo his boss was carrying. He kept saying "Diamonds!" through the gag.

"If I take that gag off, you'd better not make a row," said Gaby menacingly. "Otherwise I'll make sure you shut up, know what I mean?" He raised his fist and put it close to Dessy's face. Dessy nodded. "OK, take it off," Gaby told Larry. Larry undid the gag.

"That rope stinks," said Dessy.

"Never mind that," said Gaby. "What do you know about diamonds?"

"I know the ones you've got on board now aren't real," said Dessy.

"What? Don't be ridiculous!"

"Your friend Lavinia switched them," said Dessy.

"Lavinia? Nonsense! Call her, Larry. We'll soon sort out this lying little toe-rag."

"I haven't seen her, boss. Not since we set sail."

"Find her!" Gaby commanded. Larry went off to look for her, while Gaby called out her name several times. Then he stared at Dessy. "Stay right here!" he said.

"No problem," said Dessy, indicating his tied hands. Gaby went across to the stairs that led to the stateroom and went down them.

Larry came back on to the deck, saying: "There's no sign of her, boss." He looked around for Gaby, who at that moment rushed back up the stairs, shouting and cursing. He was holding the red box. He dipped his hand into it and picked some objects out, then let them trickle back into the box.

"Glass!" he screamed. "Bits of broken glass! That bitch! She's doublecrossed me."

"Looks that way," said Dessy.

"Shut up!" said Gaby. "I'm going to find that two-timing cow, and when I do, she'll swing for this!" He shouted to the crewman at the wheel: "Turn around. We're going back to shore."

"If you let me go, captain," said Dessy, "I can show you where to find the real diamonds, and Lavinia."

"You know where they are?" cried Gaby. He knelt down and grabbed Dessy by the throat. "Come on, talk!"

"When we're safely back on land, then I'll talk," said Dessy. He tried to sound brave, but he knew he was playing a dangerous game. When Gaby Grantham was really angry, he could do anything. Dessy thought he certainly wouldn't like to be in Lavinia's place, when Gaby caught up with her.

* * *

"They're coming back to land," said Emma Delaney, as they watched the *Merry Midas* heading towards them. "We won't need this motor launch now. He must have seen sense."

"More likely he's seen some fake diamonds," said Brendan to Molly, guessing what must have happened. "Dessy is a smart fellow."

The guards were ready on the pier when the boat docked. Gaby pushed Dessy ahead of him towards the gap in the rail where they could get off.

"You see, he's quite safe," said Gaby. Then he leaned down to whisper in Dessy's ear: "Now, lad, tell me."

"Try the ruined castle at Ballygandon," said Dessy, "but you'd better hurry."

Gaby pushed him ahead on to the pier.

"Are you all right?" asked Emma Delaney.

"Hunky-dory!" said Dessy.

"You see, guard, he's fine," said Gaby Grantham.

"So it seems," said Emma. "Now if you could just answer a few questions, Mr Grantham. We understand you were carrying some goods . . . "

"Sorry, can't stop!" said Gaby, pushing past them and hurrying up the pier. He saw Jim Shanahan and his driver, standing beside their limousine.

"Well, Gaby, I'll say goodbye then," said Jim Shanahan, holding out his hand. He was still clutching the album.

"Goodbye, Jim!" said Gaby. "I'm borrowing your car,

right?" He got into the driving seat of the limousine, and before Jim Shanahan or the driver could stop him, he was roaring away up the road.

"We know where he's heading," Locky told the guards. "Let me lead the way."

"Give us the location," said Emma. "We'll get there faster."

Brendan told her.

Locky and the Ballygandon Gang, with Tina, clambered into Pat O'Hara's car, and they followed the police car which was speeding away after the limousine towards Ballygandon. As they drove away they could hear Jim Shanahan, left behind, calling out: "Hey! What about *me?*"

* * *

On the way to Ballygandon, Brendan's father said he had been in touch with his office, and there had indeed been a theft of a large haul of diamonds from the European head-quarters of a big jewellery firm. The getaway car had been tracked to one of the ports on the English Channel, but after that the trail went cold, though there were rumours in the port of a motor cruiser heading out to sea, in the direction of Jade Island.

"It all links up," said Molly. "That's where Gaby Grantham took the *Merry Midas*. He must have had a rendezvous there to pick up the diamonds."

"He'd have been back in Dublin long ago, and offloaded them to someone, if Jim Shanahan hadn't made him come to Lough Gandon," said Dessy.

133

"And that gave Lavinia the chance to steal them from *him*," said Locky. "She's got a big headstart on us – she and Mrs O'Rourke might have got the box from the castle and skedaddled by now."

*   *   *

As they climbed the stony path up to the castle, it looked as if Locky might be right. The guards had found the ministerial limousine at the bottom of the hill, but there was no sign of Gaby Grantham. They began to make the trek up the hill, followed by Brendan's father and the Ballygandon Gang. They came to the outer wall and the guards signalled them to stop and wait. They all crouched below the outer wall.

In the courtyard inside, they could hear Gaby Grantham stamping about and calling: "OK, Lavinia, the game's up! You can't get away. Hand them over!"

There was a pause. They could hear no sound except the whistling of the wind through the ruins.

Then Gaby said: "The diamonds are no use to you, Lavinia. You don't know how to offload them, and if you don't give them to me, I'll shop you to the guards."

There was another silence. Then Gaby said: "OK, this is your last chance, Lavinia. Come out now with the diamonds, and I'll give you a share. We've still time to get away."

Molly whispered: "If we creep round the wall that way, we can get into the courtyard and get to the entrance to the tower without being seen. Then we can find out if the box is already gone."

Locky waited with the guards and Brendan's father outside the wall, distracting them while the Ballygandon Gang slipped away. Before long they were at a gap in the wall, and crawled through it, bending low as they made their way to the tower. Peering through a gap in the stones, they could see Gaby Grantham in the main courtyard, pacing about. He looked furious. Then they noticed something in his hand. It was a gun.

Molly whispered to Brendan: "I'm sure he'll use that, if he ever finds Lavinia."

"She doesn't seem to be here," said Brendan. "They must have already skipped with the loot."

"Sssh, listen!" Dessy whispered. By now they had reached the bottom of the stairway that led up into the tower. They listened. From somewhere up in the tower they could hear a strange sound. It was like somebody moaning and whimpering gently. Then they heard a voice say: "Go on. Go on down!"

Another voice replied: "I can't! She's there, at the bottom of the stairs. It's horrible!"

They recognised the voices. The first was Mrs O'Rourke's. The second was Lavinia's. Molly and Brendan peered round the corner of the arch. Halfway up the stairs they could see Lavinia, crouching down and trembling. She was pointing to the bottom of the stairs. "Look, look! Oh, it's ghastly!" she screamed. "Get away! Get away!"

They all looked where she was pointing, but could see nothing.

Behind Lavinia, Mrs O'Rourke said: "There's nothing there. Give me the box and I'll go down."

"No. . . no . . . " Lavinia was crying now.

"Give it to me!" There was a scuffle on the stairs, and they saw Mrs O'Rourke stumble down them, clutching the box. At the bottom, she gave a loud scream and clutched at her throat. She began to writhe, shouting: "Let go! Let go!" Then with a final piercing screech she fell to the ground unconscious. The box fell from her hands, its lid coming off. A cascade of gleaming diamonds scattered on to the ground.

They could see Lavinia crouching up on the stairs behind. "Let me out, let me out!" she whimpered.

Suddenly Gaby Grantham lurched towards them.

"I heard you!" he yelled triumphantly. He dashed past them and saw the diamonds at the bottom of the stairs, and the figure of Mrs O'Rourke lying unconscious beside them. He knelt down and began to scoop the diamonds up and put them into the box. Then he gave a scream of pain and clutched at his throat. He too began writhing and fell to the ground.

Up in the tower they could hear Lavinia crying: "Let me go. Let me go . . ."

They looked up into the tower, where they could see the strange violet glowing light they had seen before. It began to fade and then get brighter again. Then there was a final flash of bright light, like an explosion, and they heard what sounded like a cackle of laughter.

There was a silence, and then Lavinia came rolling and tumbling down the stairs. She landed at the bottom and sat there, gasping.

The guards with Locky and Brendan's father came across the courtyard. Lavinia and the others offered no resistance as the guards handcuffed them. One of the guards picked up the box and began putting the remaining diamonds back into it.

Brendan produced his camera and took a picture of the scene. "That'll be front page news all right!" said Brendan's father. "Well done! You've all done a fantastic job."

As he talked to the guards, Brendan turned to Molly and Dessy with the camera.

"It's a pity we won't be able to see the main character in all this, even though Lavinia saw her all right," Brendan said, as he held the camera out for Molly and Dessy to look.

The three of them gazed at the picture and felt a chill come over them. Could it just be a trick of the light, or was the shadowy figure of Princess Ethna there at the bottom of the stairs . . ?

The End